THE SEAL'S SURPRISE RESCUE (SPECIAL FORCES: OPERATION ALPHA)

RACHEL MCNEELY

Dear Readers,

Welcome to the Special Forces: Operation Alpha Fan-Fiction world!

If you are new to this amazing world, in a nutshell the author wrote a story using one or more of my characters in it. Sometimes that character has a major role in the story, and other times they are only mentioned briefly. This is perfectly legal and allowable because they are going through Aces Press to publish the story.

This book is entirely the work of the author who wrote it. While I might have assisted with brainstorming and other ideas about which of my characters to use, I didn't have any part in the process or writing or editing the story.

I'm proud and excited that so many authors loved my characters enough that they wanted to write them into their own story. Thank you for supporting them, and me!

READ ON!

Xoxo

Susan Stoker

CHAPTER 1

Madison Carney smiled across the dining room table at his friend, Dirk Foster, better known on their SEAL team as Ranger. "I'm glad you and Haley were free to join me tonight. I wanted to congratulate both of you on your marriage, although how you convinced this pretty, smart lady to marry you, Ranger, is a puzzle to me."

Ranger laughed and took hold of Haley's hand. "She led me down a merry path with lots of excitement and almost killed me. I think she married me because she believed she needed to be around to keep me safe."

Haley's face turned tomato red. Ranger leaned over and kissed her.

"Is half of what Ranger said true?"

"I'm afraid so. You'll have to come to dinner, and we'll tell you the whole story." Haley blew a kiss at Ranger.

"Dear me, I never thought I'd see Ranger so enamored with any lady."

Ranger grinned and nodded his head toward Madison, telling Haley, "Madison is the intellectual one of the group. Most of us don't use such fancy words, as you might have noticed. Madison likes to disappear and go home to read."

"There's nothing wrong with enjoying quiet time and reading," Haley said.

"Nope, and he's a great medic. We used to call him Doc, but later changed it to Professor because he's so smart."

"I'm just a medic, but I answer to whatever they call me. Would you all like to order dessert?"

"No, I think we'll head home. But thanks for the meal." Ranger stood and pulled out Haley's chair. "I'm glad you got back from taking care of your Dad and will join us on Monday. We've missed you."

"I'm happy to be back. I think I'll sit here and finish my coffee before I leave."

After the happy couple left, Madison sipped his coffee and glanced around the room. His eyes connected with those of a woman sitting several tables over. Her auburn hair shimmered in the light above her head. When she smiled, his heart skipped a beat.

Damn, she's a beauty, but not for me. Madison remembered the mistakes he'd made in his first marriage, and he planned to stay away from getting involved for quite a while. He took the last swallow of his coffee, paid the bill, and headed for the door.

I lucked out when I got the last parking space in front of the restaurant. I won't have to walk far. I hope I haven't gotten out of shape and lazy while away.

As the door swung shut at his back, Madison took three long steps toward his vehicle. And stopped. A man was bent over the driver's-side door.

"What the hell do you think you're doing?" Madison grabbed the man by the back of his collar, swung him around, and punched him.

The guy barreled into Madison, and Madison wrestled with him for control. With a hard punch in the belly and chin, the would-be-robber fell back. Red in the face and angry, he got up to fight again. When he moved forward, he tripped and fell against Madison, taking them both down.

"Damn, that hurt." Madison rubbed his head and tried to blink his eyes to clear his vision. He heard someone shout.

"Drop the gun!" Two guns went off simultaneously.

Madison tried to focus his eyes. *Damn, what a time to have trouble seeing his rescuer.* No matter how much he blinked, he saw double. He thought he saw two women of Amazonian proportions, then he blacked out.

* * *

Kathleen Cafferty, better known as Kat, leaned over the handsome man she'd admired in the restaurant. When her party left, she'd hurried out the door, hoping to see him again.

She didn't expect to find a fight and for him to be involved. She heard a man tell another bystander that the guy who'd got up and stood over the fallen one had tried to steal his car.

When the thief pulled a gun, Kat had yelled, "Police! Drop your gun, or I'll have to shoot you!"

Instead, the man whirled in her direction, gun pointed at her. She leaned to the left and shot at him. His bulled missed her by an inch. The guy with the gun had a bullet in his chest. Kat called for two ambulances and back-up.

"I'm a doctor," a man said from behind her. I'll check them both until the ambulance arrives." He hurried to the man with the bleeding chest, and a lady came running with a black bag.

Breathless, she said, "Here, honey," and handed the Samaritan the bag. The women turned to check on the handsome man just as he came around.

"I'm fine," he told her.

"Maybe, maybe not. You may have a concussion. I'm a nurse, and I happened to be inside the restaurant with my husband, who's a doctor. He's working on the man shot in the chest. Let me check your pupils." She shined a small penlight into his eyes. "Both are reacting to light, but you may be admitted and watched for the next twenty-four hours."

"No way. I'm a medic. I can take care of myself."

"Are you one of those foolish medical people who don't take good medical advice?" she asked with a smile. She looked around and nodded to Kat. "This lady happens to be a police officer. She saved your life."

* * *

Madison looked up and blinked. "Are there two Amazons standing over me?"

Kat laughed. "No, just one."

"Damn fine woman looking at me," he mumbled. "Sorry, did I say damn?"

"You're excused this time."

"I remember you from the restaurant. A beautiful fantasy, but not for me."

"Sorry to hear that. I kind of liked the looks of you, too." Kat grinned. The blow to his head had affected his thinking and words. When he recovered, she bet he'd be embarrassed by what he said.

"Who's the lady who just left?"

"Her husband's a doctor, and she's a nurse. I've met them before at this restaurant. Nice people and ready to help when needed." She looked closer when she finished talking and realized he'd gone out again.

"I guess no questions for you until tomorrow." She straightened and saw the ambulances come around the corner.

Several men jumped out and hurried to where the man with the chest injury lay. They got a quick report from the doctor, loaded the patient on a stretcher, and left with sirens blaring. The other ambulance stopped near Madison. Medics hurried across the walkway to check on him.

"He's in and out of consciousness. When he fell, he must have hit the side of his head on the curb. I see a lump forming," Kat said.

She took a deep breath as they quickly checked his injuries and the rest of him to see if he had any other problems. Usually, she'd rush over to question bystanders, but she couldn't leave his side until the one EMT had checked Madison's pulse and blood pressure.

"He's stable. We'll get him to the emergency room fast. They can check him more thoroughly, and his pockets to find out who to call."

"All right. I'll go to the hospital later. I'm Detective Cafferty. Here's my card if you need to contact me."

"Thanks." The ambulance driver dropped it in his pocket as they hurried to put Madison in the ambulance.

Kat watched as the vehicle drove off. *What a night. My brothers will love this story, and I am eager to see the victim early tomorrow.*

* * *

The phone rang while Ranger kissed Haley. He ignored it for a moment, but when it kept ringing, he leaned away from her and grabbed the phone. "Hello," he snapped.

Captain Buchanan chuckled. "I must have called at a bad time."

"Sorry, Captain. I thought I had another robocall."

"I'm contacting you because I got a call from the downtown hospital emergency room. They said Madison had arrived with a head injury. I believe they're considering keeping him tonight to make sure he's going to be all right."

"What? We left him at the restaurant about an hour and a half ago."

"I know you mentioned he'd invited you and Haley to dinner. That's why I'm calling."

"Yes. He wanted to sit and finish his coffee before he left. I don't know what happened afterward."

"I didn't expect you would, or you'd have called me. Do you mind going to the emergency room and letting me know how Madison ended up injured? If he doesn't get discharged in the morning, we'll need to get him transferred to Balboa Military hospital."

"I'll check it all out, Captain, and call you back."

"Thanks. I know you two are close. I thought Madison might prefer to see your face than mine."

"I'm on my way." Ranger ended the call and turned to Haley. "I have no idea what happened, but Madison is in the emergency room. I need to go check on him. It's late. Why don't you go to bed, and I'll wake you when I get home."

"I see that sparkle in your eye. You'd better not disappoint me. I doubt I'll sleep much worrying about Madison. Call and let me know how he's doing."

Ranger pulled her tight against him and kissed her. "I will. Got to go." He rushed out to the garage and tried not to speed as he headed downtown. *Hell. What happened in such a short period?*

* * *

Once he'd found a parking space close to the emergency entrance, Ranger ran across the pavement and through the doors.

A receptionist standing at the desk yelled out, "Slow

down, Sir! You need to check in before you go any further."

"Sorry, I'm looking for Madison Carney. He came in by ambulance."

"Sure, we all know who you're talking about. He's behind the curtain in Cubicle Three. You'll have to sign in and wait. The doctor's checking him over now."

"How do you and everyone know who Madison is other than his name?" Ranger asked with a frown.

She grinned. "Because he's a handsome hunk like you."

Ranger seldom blushed. The nurse laughed at his red face. "You must be used to women letting you know that you're handsome."

"Our wives tell us often."

"Darn, you're married."

"I am and happy to be."

The woman sighed, then said, "I see your friend's doctor heading this way. Dr. Roberts, this is Mr. Carney's friend."

"I'm glad you're here. Mr. Carney had two cards in his pocket, one identifying his parents and one for the officer the head nurse spoke with earlier."

"Our Captain called and asked me to check on Madison. How is he?"

"He got a hard smack on his head, but the X-rays showed no fractures or bleeds. I want to keep him overnight, just to be on the safe side. If everything checks out in the morning, he'll be discharged."

"Can I see him?"

"Yes. Your friend may be a bit confused at times, but

by morning, his mind should be clear, or we'll do more tests. I'm sending him up to the neuro floor for head injuries."

"You have a special floor for those types of injuries?"

"It's small, but we do tend to see more injuries with everyone paying more attention to their phones and other electronic devices than on what they're doing. And most all of them need follow-up and checks every hour, at least the first night."

"Thanks, Dr. Roberts. I'll check on him and call my Captain to let him know Madison is doing fine, for now." Ranger strode toward the indicated cubicle.

"I knew you'd get in trouble by yourself," Ranger teased when Madison opened his eyes. "The Captain's worried about you."

Madison squinted. "Ranger, why do I see two of you?"

"The doctor said you were better. I guess you'll need to be transferred to Balboa in the morning if you continue to see me in double."

Madison laughed. "One of you is enough. Please take me home in the morning."

"I will if the Captain says it's okay. The world can't handle two of me," Ranger said and grinned. "Do you remember what happened?"

"Some, but other parts are sketchy."

"Tell me what you remember. I'll need to explain to Captain Buchanan."

Madison told him about catching the guy messing with his car. "After I hit the curb, everything got somewhat confusing. Gunshots went off, and later a beautiful

Amazon woman checked on me. If I remember right, she had a gun on her hip. It may have been her who shot the would-be thief."

"An Amazon?" Ranger raised his eyebrows. "I hope your memory is better by morning or you'll be transferred to Balboa."

"I'm telling you the truth."

"Okay, don't get upset. I'll be back in the morning to pick you up. Be good."

Madison laughed, then winced. "Oh, that hurt a bit. Most of the time, I'm the one telling you to be good."

"I know, but my beautiful wife has tamed me. Well, just a bit." Ranger winked, waved, and headed out of the hospital toward home. *When I call the Captain, I'll leave out the part about the Amazon.*

* * *

Kat chuckled to herself as she strapped on her holster and secured her gun. Thoughts of the handsome man stretched out on the sidewalk had flashed in her mind several times since last night, which wasn't like her. She'd been off men since her divorce from her high school sweetheart.

I'll see how he affects me when I visit him this morning. Kat's cell rang. She grabbed it, answering when her brother's name flashed on the screen.

"Hi, Kat," Scott said. "I just read your report from yesterday evening. Looks like you walked into the altercation."

"I did. Two men were fighting. I watched for a

minute, and one guy pulled a gun. I warned him I'd have to shoot. He turned and fired, missing me by an inch or so, but I got him. I'm headed to the hospital to see how he's doing and check on the other man."

"I called this morning and checked on the man you shot. He's going to be hospitalized for at least a week, but the doctor thinks he'll live to go to trial."

"That's good news. I'm headed to check on the other man, the one he pulled the gun on. I'll ask him what started it all."

"Good. Keep in touch. See you later at the precinct."

Kat clicked off her phone and headed out the door. *I've never been so eager to see a victim before. I hope my reaction will be different today.* But she smiled as she thought about him calling her an Amazon.

"Damn," Kat muttered when she saw all the parking spaces near the hospital entrance filled. There were two spots reserved for police cars, but she didn't like to use them for a regular visit. Another police officer might need the place for an emergency. *Walking will be good for me.*

As she took long strides toward the door, warm air blew across her. Thank goodness detectives got to wear regular clothes. They were lighter in weight than uniforms.

After checking at reception for Mr. Carney's room number, she headed to the elevators. Once on the seventh floor, she spoke with the nurse at the desk.

"How's Mr. Carney doing?"

"Much better. We're waiting for the physician. He'll be discharged today unless the doctor finds a problem.

We hate to see him go. He's a nice man. And handsome," the nurse said and grinned.

"Yes, that's the impression I got. I'll be in Mr. Carney's room. I have some questions for him."

"Lucky you. The few times his light came on, the nurses fought for who'd answer," she said and laughed.

Hmm. So I'm not the only one to find him handsome.

Kat knocked on his door.

"Come in."

As soon as she entered the room and he spotted her, he smiled.

"I dreamed about the beautiful Amazon who saved my life. You are real."

"Yes, but last time I checked, I was a detective and work for our local police."

"I saw you in the restaurant. You smiled back at me."

"Something I don't normally do."

"Why not? You have a lovely smile."

"Long story. I have some questions for you, Mr. Carney. What started the fight?"

"He tried to break into my car. When I yanked him away, the fight started. I'm embarrassed. I'd have had him down in a few minutes, but the guy had a good swing. Stronger than expected. A little over a month away from work, and I've gotten out of shape."

Kat shook her head. "You look strong. I think he got a lucky blow in, and the curb took care of the rest."

"I like your version."

"I noticed on the chart that you're in the Navy."

"Yes, ma'am."

She grimaced.

"What's wrong?"

"Ma'am sounds old. How about calling me Detective Cafferty."

"Cafferty. That name sounds familiar, but I'm sure if we'd met, I wouldn't have forgotten you."

Kat cleared her throat. "Shall we get back to business? Had you ever seen the man before?"

"No, and I'm surprised he didn't run when I jerked him away from my car. If I remember right, you shot him."

"Yes, but he's doing okay right now."

"Good. I'm glad the man didn't die."

"Why?"

"In my job ..." Madison stopped. He mustn't say too much. "I expect both of us didn't want him to die over trying to steal a car. I wonder why he looked so desperate?"

"Thieving is his profession. He knows the risk. The rest is your imagination."

"Maybe, but I believe I'm right, and I want to find out the truth. When I glanced into the robber's eyes, he looked desperate. Would you check about his family?"

"Some other police officer will do that, and hospital personnel will also have contacted his family."

Madison shook his head and grimaced when it hurt worse. "I'll visit his hospital room before leaving. Hopefully, some family will be with him."

"I don't believe you'll be allowed to see him. You aren't family. What did you expect to find?"

"I don't know, but I feel I must talk with him and his significant others."

A man stuck his head inside the doorway. "Hi. Am I interrupting?"

"Ranger, come on in. This is my Amazon rescuer from last night. Detective Cafferty, this is one of my best friends, Dirk Foster, better known as Ranger."

"Ah, I thought you were still confused." Kat had stood, and Ranger smiled at her. "Madison's not wrong. You are a beautiful Amazon."

"What is this Amazon thing with you two?"

"We're all tall and to find a pretty lady like you, with your stature, doesn't often happen. Not that our shorter wives aren't gorgeous, too."

"Good save, in the rare chance I ever meet the wives."

"Oh, I think it might happen." He winked at Madison.

"You've said enough, Ranger. Have I been discharged?"

"The nurse at the desk said yes, after you sign your discharge papers. I've come to get you, but Captain Buchanan wants you checked over at Balboa before I take you home. If you're all right, he expects you to report tomorrow morning."

"I gather you're Navy, too," Kat said.

"Yes."

"I may have more questions. I'll call if I do."

"Thanks for checking on me," Madison said.

"I always visit victims to get their side of the story," Kat said as she hurried out the door.

* * *

"She's going to be a tough nut to crack."

"What makes you think I'm interested in her, Ranger?"

"You have *the* look. You might as well give up now."

"I think you're touched in the head." Changing the subject, he said, "Before I allow you to take me out of this place, we're going to see the man who shot me and talk with him."

"Why?"

"I think he had a serious reason to try to steal a car."

"You're confused. The man who tried to rip off your car is a thief. I'm sure a police officer is sitting outside his door."

"Just do as I ask, please."

"All right. I have a wheelchair outside your door and we'll sign you out. How do we find this guy's room?"

"The nurse will tell us."

His nurse smiled when Ranger rolled Madison up to the desk. "Thanks for all the good care you and the other staff gave me during my stay," Madison said to the nurse and the receptionist sitting nearby.

"No problem. You were a great patient."

Ranger snorted behind him. Madison cast a glance at his friend. "See? I told you they liked me."

Looking back to the nurse, he asked, "Can you tell me the room number where they put the man who shot me?"

"I can't. The patient is in ICU anyway." She put her hand to her mouth as if to take back the admission. "I shouldn't have told you. Don't go up and cause a disturbance."

"Don't worry. I'm not going to cause trouble. I'm concerned about his family. I expect I can see them in the waiting room."

"Is he for real?" the nurse asked Ranger.

"Yeah, the rest of us aren't as nice. Don't worry, Mr. Carney won't hurt anyone."

"Okay."

When they got on the elevator, Ranger whispered, "She's worried."

"I'm sorry, but I want to speak with whoever is in the waiting room for him."

CHAPTER 2

Shrugging, Ranger wheeled Madison off on the fifth floor and down the hall on the left, where a sign pointed them to the ICU waiting room. Inside, they found an older woman and a younger one.

Madison asked, "Are either of you relatives of the man admitted with a gunshot wound last night?"

The younger woman looked up. "Yes. I'm Karen, his wife, and this is his mother, Mrs. Kesler. Who are you?"

"I'm the man he fought with last night. He tried to steal my car."

Mrs. Kesler seemed to pale and started to cry. "I raised Philip to be a good boy. He's never done anything like this before."

Karen reached for her mother-in-law as tears began to stream down her own face.

"I believe you. I saw a frantic look in your son's eyes. Why did he want to steal a car?"

For a Moment, Karen only shook her head and cried harder. When she regained some control, she gulped and said, "It's because of our daughter. She's in this same hospital on the fourth floor. She's sick and needs some special treatment. I think he hoped to get enough money so we can move to where she's being flown for treatment. He's had difficulty getting a job that pays enough to feed us and pay the rent. I don't know what we'll do now."

"Don't worry. I'll get help for you. Does your husband have a lawyer?"

"No, but they said when he's better, they'll have a lawyer assigned to him."

"I have a friend. She's a good attorney, but she's a prosecutor. I'll talk to her about help for your husband."

Brokenly, she asked, "Why are you helping us?"

"His look of desperation won't get out of my mind." Madison smiled sadly at the young woman and her mother-in-law. "Have you got a paper to write down your name and number? I will get back to you."

With nervous hands, the wife scribbled down her name and cell phone number and handed the slip of paper over. "I hope you can read it."

"I can, Karen. I'll call you soon."

He waved at the women as Ranger pushed him out of the room and they headed toward the elevator. In the empty elevator, Ranger asked, "Are you crazy?"

"Maybe, but did you know what's been going on with my family the past month?"

Ranger said slowly, "A family emergency, that's all the Captain would say, and not to ask you about it until you were ready."

"My father had heart surgery, and someone donated

a heart that replaced his worn-out one. I didn't tell anyone but the Captain. He understood why I needed to be with Mom and Dad." Madison shrugged. "This is my way of paying back."

"Helping a man who tried to rob you and knocked you out?"

"I'm out of shape. I hang my head in shame that I didn't get him out first."

"You're avoiding the question."

"You heard his wife and mother. I am paying back a good man who went wrong for the right reasons. My guess is they'd already maxed out all the help available."

Ranger shook his head as the elevator door opened on the ground floor. "How you ever got tough enough to be a SEAL is a wonder to me."

"Oh, I don't mind being tough on the real bad guys if I'm not busy trying to tend my team members who get hurt."

"Yeah. When necessary, you fight as good as any of us."

"Of course." Madison smiled at Ranger. "Take me home."

"Nope, Balboa. You have to be checked okay for duty first, and only then home."

* * *

When Madison stepped into his house, he took a deep breath and released it, closed his eyes and let the peacefulness flow through him. He'd had his house for seven years. Coming home to it always relaxed him, no matter what had occurred in the previous days.

In the kitchen, he put on the coffee before strolling out to the backyard. The wind rippled the water in his pool. He decided he'd put on his swimsuit, bring his coffee out here, and then later lay on his couch in the den to read.

Tomorrow he'd be back at work. He looked forward to his life, settling down, returning to the regular routine.

He changed, got his coffee, took a sip, and placed his cup on the outside table by his pool. His cell rang just when he walked to the edge of his pool to dive in.

Damn, I ought to turn off the phone. "Hello," he snapped.

"Do you have a headache from your incident?"

The cool, sexy, feminine voice sent heat racing through his body.

"Sorry, no, I don't. Your call stopped me before I got to jump in my pool, Detective."

"Ah, too bad. You didn't have time to answer my questions earlier, and I bet you'll be at work tomorrow."

"You're right."

"May I come by your house and talk to you?"

"Yes. I have an idea I'd like to tell you about and get your opinion."

"Only if you answer my questions first."

"Agreed."

"I have your address. I'm only ten minutes away."

"You weren't going to take no for an answer."

"I never do."

"Wow, a tough lady. Come on by, and I'll have a tall, cold glass of tea waiting."

"That's bribery I can accept," the Detective said and hung up.

Madison grinned as he clicked off his phone. *I've got to be careful. I like her too much already.*

When the doorbell rang, he greeted her with the tea. "Hope you like it. Made it myself."

She took a sip. Madison watched her expression closely and smiled when she took several sips.

"I was thirsty. This hit the spot. Now I'm ready to get my questions answered."

* * *

She'd gulped the tea to keep him from noticing her expression. The man would take any woman's breath away. His swimming trunks left his arms, chest and legs exposed, showing off his tan, lots of bulging muscles and a washboard belly. When he smiled, her heartbeat raced.

Her brother had given her his information. She'd noted his occupation, Navy SEAL. His deep voice and light-blue eyes were the final detail to make him any woman's dream.

"Where would you like to sit while you interrogate me?" he asked. "It's nice outside. I have a good bit of shade in my yard."

"That sounds good."

He walked beside her as they strolled through a

family room and out onto the patio. "Your home is lovely, but isn't it rather large for a single man?"

"My ex-wife liked the space. I do, too. She wanted a condo after she left and I stayed in the house."

"I might have stayed for the house. It has an air of quiet peace. After I come home from my job, it's exactly what I need."

"I agree. We both work in demanding jobs. Most people need a place to relax." Madison grinned. "Some SEALs may not agree with me, but my team is all married now, except me. They're just now finding out how to enjoy and relax at home."

He motioned to a patio chair and pulled it out for her. "The sun won't be in your eyes sitting here, and I'll sit beside you. What do you want to ask me?"

"Are you certain that you never saw the man who attacked you before the other night?"

"Never, and I want to discuss him with you."

"Even though you were the victim, I can't say much."

"No problem, but I'll tell you what I have in mind. Number one, I don't want to prosecute him."

She sat straighter in her chair. "Well, I do. The guy almost hit me with a bullet."

"Let me tell you why he looked desperate." Madison explained what he knew about the family. "He was in a corner, and his family depended on him. I'm not saying what he did was right, but I want to help the family and get them out of the hole they're in right now."

"What do you have in mind?"

"A few ways to help is to get them to the city where their daughter is being transferred for some type of special treatment. They need help getting there and finding a place to stay. He needs an attorney. It's his first offense, according to his wife, Karen."

She laughed. "You are gullible if you believe he hasn't tried to steal before now."

"Do you have evidence of previous robberies?"

She frowned at him and stayed silent.

Madison grinned. "You don't."

"I can't tell you yea or nay."

"The same here. I have no more information about what happened. You have all I know written down."

"Maybe, but I think there's more to this generosity than you've told me."

"You are a suspicious woman. Perhaps it's required in your job. But the world is full of good people who want to help others. Recently, my father got another chance at life. Someone signed a donor card, and that person's heart is beating in my Dad's chest. I want to pay it forward."

"You can do that by signing your own donor card."

"I did a long time ago. No, whatever you say won't change my mind about helping this family."

She stood. "You're a strange man. But let me tell you, there is no way he's not going to be tried and most probably found guilty. California has strong gun laws, and he shot at a police officer and barely missed." Kat turned and strode through the living room to the door.

"You don't have to hurry off."

"Yes, I do. There are other people to talk with today."

"If you ever have any free time, give me a call, and I'll

take you to dinner. A thank you for saving my life and an opportunity to learn more about you."

He handed her his card. "I may be out of town for work, but leave a message. I'll call back as soon as possible."

His large hand enveloped hers. "I'd like to help you see the better side of people."

When he opened the front door for her, she rushed out. "Thank you for your time." As quickly as her heels would let her walk, she hurried to the unmarked car parked near the front of his house.

Kat sat for a moment to catch her breath. She glanced in the rear-view mirror and saw he still stood watching her car. He was a handsome man and dangerous to her heart. Determined to put him out of her mind, she drove off.

* * *

Madison watched until her vehicle turned and moved swiftly out of sight. *She's a prickly lady and doesn't give an inch. She'd be hard to live with.* That gave him pause. *What brought on that thought?*

As he walked back into the house, his cell rang. He checked the name on the screen and answered, "Hi, Captain."

"How are you feeling?"

"Like I'm ready to get back to work. It's good to hear your voice."

"I saw Ranger at the store, and he told me your idea

to help the family of the man who tried to steal your car and then shot at the police officer."

"Most people like Ranger and the lady detective think my brain is still damaged."

"My wife loves your idea. I'm going to let her get on the phone and tell you how she and her club would like to help."

"Sounds great. Thanks."

After a Moment, another voice spoke in his ear. "Hi, Madison, this is Emma. I'm a member of a women's club, and with the holidays coming soon, we've been trying to think of how we might help a family."

"This man's family needs a lot of help."

"I understand. We're having a meeting tomorrow night at seven. I'd like you to join us and let others hear what is needed. Then we can decide how we might help you meet your goal."

"No problem. Send me the address and phone number and I'll be there." Madison hesitated. "Would you mind if I brought the wife with me?"

"I think that's a great idea."

"I'll call her and see if she'll let me drive her to your meeting."

"She may hesitate. How many times have you met her?"

"Once, when I got her phone number."

"Let me call her. I'll suggest we all go together. You can come and get me, and then we'll go to her place."

"It may be a homeless shelter."

"No problem. If so, we'll know that this lady needs us to help quickly."

Madison recited Karen Kesler's number. "Let me know how it works out with her."

"Will do."

* * *

It was family night at the Cafferty house. Kat found a place to park between two of her brothers' cars. She'd taken time to go home and change, so from the looks of the vehicles parked outside, she was the last to arrive.

Kat took a deep breath when she walked into her mother's kitchen. The smell of herbs and spices filled the air.

"How are you, Mom?" she asked and bent to kiss the smallest person in the family.

Her mother stopped stirring and put a lid on the pot. She stepped in front of her daughter and looked her over from head to feet. "I hear you almost got shot the other night."

"Ah, Mom, you know I'm the best one in the group for ducking."

"And shooting at the same time, from what I hear." Her Mom lowered her voice. "Your Dad and the boys are proud of you, but they'll heckle you rather than admit it."

"I know, Mom. It's their way of showing love."

Her mother nodded. "Oh, and by the way, Tammy is pregnant."

"What? The twins are six years old. I thought Gavin and Tammy weren't planning on any more for fear of having another set of twins."

"I guess your brother and Tammy decided to give it a try. They're hoping for a boy."

"Ah, yes, to carry on the Cafferty name."

Her Mom laughed. "As if with three brothers and three nephews, that wasn't enough. Go on in the living room and join them."

"Can't I help?"

"Nope. A few more minutes, and it'll be all done. Deirdre already volunteered, but you can help next family night."

As if the sound of her name summoned her, Kat's sister entered the kitchen and gave her a hug. "Hi, Kat." She towed her into the family room. "Scott just told us about you almost being shot last night and, more importantly, that the man you saved happened to be a Navy SEAL. Cory couldn't get away from his training tonight, but I wonder if our little brother has met your guy."

All the family had turned to face Kat. *Damn, my face is red. I can feel it. Here comes the teasing.*

Taking a breath and trying to appear nonchalant, Kat said, "He's not *my* SEAL. If he hadn't knocked his head on the curb, I wouldn't have been needed."

"You took out the guy before he shot the SEAL," Scott reminded her.

"True."

Did you go to his house today?" Scott asked.

"Yes, I did. He's met the family and feels sorry for them, and he said he was dropping his charges. I reminded him I'd almost took a bullet and had no plans to let him go free."

"How'd he take your comments?" her sister asked.

"The man's too nice. I don't know how he functions as a SEAL. I mean, he's a medic, but while we were talking I gathered he does all the same duties as his buddies unless he's working on one of them."

"Our brother is nice, and he's just become a SEAL," Lloyd, her brother, who was a medical intern, reminded Kat.

Their mother had stepped into the room in time to hear Lloyd's comment.

"I'd never have thought the son who never wanted to get up in the morning and hated chores would pass the SEAL test. I must admit we all ought to be happy for him. Supper is ready. Go to the table and, Deirdre, you can help me bring in the food from the kitchen."

* * *

Kat let herself into her apartment and turned on the lights, locked the door, and went into the kitchen. All the conversation at the table tonight had been about Tammy's pregnancy and Kat's close call.

I had difficulty not letting them know how the handsome SEAL affects me. She had blushed once, but her brothers had started another conversation and thankfully didn't notice. *Still, my sister and several sisters-in-law saw my reaction. I hope they won't tell my brothers.*

After drinking a glass of water, Kat headed to her bedroom. It was eight-thirty. *I'll shower and, with some luck, I can finish reading my book tonight.* When she placed her beeper on the bedside table, she said, "Be quiet, no business tonight." She knew the chances of that were slim. This was her week on call.

After her shower, sitting in bed reading calmed all her thoughts and took her to another place. When she clicked off the light at eleven and snuggled down in bed, she drifted off to sleep. The beeper went off.

CHAPTER 3

Kat turned off her siren and got out of the car. Police cars surrounded the large, luxurious house set in a private area and surrounded by high walls with guards.

The only information the dispatcher had was a woman died during a party. *Must have been some affair.*

She showed her ID and got escorted to a huge banquet room. A band must have been playing, but now they were busy putting their instruments into cases.

Guests dressed in fancy gowns and tuxedos wandered around, looking stunned. Kat saw her partner, Marcos Camilius, talking with a tall, broad-chested man she immediately recognized as Enzo Massito, one of the city's top crime bosses. She headed in their direction.

"Mr. Massito, this is my partner, Detective Cafferty."

The man frowned. "Your name is familiar. You have a brother on the force?"

"Possibly. Why would it matter?"

"He doesn't like me, nor do I like him."

"Interesting. What does this have to do with whatever happened tonight?"

"I don't trust him." The man leaned down closer to her.

Kat held her position. "That has nothing to do with me."

Massito straightened up and turned to Marcos. "I want another detective."

"We'll ask about it tomorrow, but for tonight, we are on call," Marcos said sternly.

"What happened, Mr. Massito?" Kat asked.

Massito spoke in an angry tone. "Someone killed my wife."

Kat bit her tongue, to keep from asking Massito if he killed his wife. Instead she quizzed him regarding he and his wife's relationship."

He placed his hand over his heart. "My Camilla was my love, my flower."

"All right. Where is your wife now?"

"We didn't move her," Marcos said. "His wife is around back, hanging from a point on one of the metal gargoyles projecting from a roof gutter in the back."

Kat took a deep breath and blinked. Then she looked at Massito. "You have gargoyles on your gutters?"

"A few," he said, and his body stiffened. "My wife had requested I have them removed, and I agreed to call someone next week to do the job."

"How convenient for the killer for them to still be here this weekend for his use."

"Maybe she wasn't killed," Massito snarled. "She might have fallen."

"Without help?" Kat asked.

"You are a very suspicious person," he said and leaned close to her face, the expression on his mean.

"Are you threatening me?" Kat asked without moving.

"Do you feel threatened by me?"

"No, but I suspect your wife had those emotions at times." Kat glanced at her partner, who was giving her the look that said she was about to push too hard. She stopped talking and imagined seeing smoke roll out of the top of Massito's head.

"Shall we go and see where your wife died?" Marcos asked.

Tears came into the other man's eyes as he turned to lead the way.

They took an elevator up to the mansion's top floor. "The whole floor is our suite. It contains the bedroom, sitting room, closets, and my office," Massito said when the elevator doors opened.

Kat blinked. The architecture was modern, but the decorations softened the harder appearance of the rooms. "I like what your designer did to these rooms," Kat said.

"My wife designed houses for a living. That's how we met."

Curtains at an open window near the bed blew inward from the breeze outside. Kat nodded toward the opening. "Is that the window from where your wife jumped or was pushed?"

"No one working for me would push her. They know their life would end shortly if they touched a hair on Camilla's head."

Kat was surprised to see tears in the man's eyes. "Perhaps she had an enemy and didn't tell you."

The change in the man startled her. He sank onto the soft bed and covered his face with his big hands. Massito's breathing became labored, and sobs gasped out of his mouth.

"Are you all right?" Kat asked. She knelt by his side.

"You don't care. From the first, you decided I had killed my wife."

"We push the wife or husband to make certain they aren't the person who killed their mate. You were angry and acted guilty."

"Do you think I'd let my men see me being soft?"

"Perhaps in this situation, I'd expect some other reaction than what you'd shown to us until now."

Marcos had walked to the window and looked out. He checked the windowsill and the floor. He turned to the husband and gestured at the floor. "Is this one of your wife's shoes?"

Mr. Massito wiped his eyes and stood unsteadily. "Yes. I remember she came up to me and whispered in my ear about going upstairs to change her shoes. She said one of them had rubbed a blister on her heel."

"What did you say?" Marcos asked, watching him closely.

"I laughed and teased her about not having many choices to choose from." He blinked his eyes and took a breath. "It was a joke between us, her love of shoes.

Never one to throw money around, but that was her one weakness. I loved to see the different shoes she'd bring home. I'd tease her, and we'd laugh." He sat back down on the side of the bed and closed his eyes. "How will I go on without her joy?"

Kat began to feel sorry for badgering Massito. *But I've never seen a crime boss with a soft spot. And there was no doubt about his reputation.*

She walked to the window where Marcos stood and surveyed the area. When their eyes met, Marcos nodded, and she said, "I agree."

"Agree about what?" Massito asked.

"Your happy wife didn't jump or accidentally fall out of this window. For one reason, the way the window is built, it isn't a good one to choose if someone wanted to go out it," Marcos said.

Then Kat said softly, "I'm sorry to tell you, Mr. Massito, but someone threw your wife out of this window."

"What?" He pushed up from the bed and rushed to the window.

"It took a strong man to heave her out in such a way to hit that gargoyle. And notice the scratches on the window seal?" Kat gestured at them. "She fought for her life."

"But who? My wife was loved by everyone. Her joy and brightness went out to all of us. The servants insisted on helping to care for her when she had the flu."

He paced across the floor and ran his fingers through his hair. "I was away, and they assured me by the time I returned, Camilla would be fine. When I got home, she couldn't stop praising them for their loving care."

"Did your wife ever mention being scared of anyone?" Kat asked.

"No." Then he stopped pacing and turned. He closed his eyes as though trying to recall something.

"When we were first married, my number one helper resented her interrupting us at times. He snapped at her once. I warned him if he ever didn't respect her and speak to her in a pleasant tone, he'd be gone. He stayed a month longer and left."

Massito hit the side of his head. "On his way out, the man dared to say I'd gone soft. I heard through the grapevine that he'd gone to another town."

"So, you're certain he couldn't have killed your wife?" Marcos asked.

For a second, Kat saw the glitter of hate in Massito's eyes. "No. He's been gone a long time. No way he'd come back to kill my precious Camilla."

"When we find the person who did this, we will arrest them, they will go to trial, and I'm confident they will receive a sentence of many years in jail," Kat said. She stared hard at Massito. "You understand what I am saying?"

A hard smile covered his face. "Perhaps. If you find the person first."

Kat wanted to say more, but decided it was useless. She knew if Massito found whoever had killed his wife, they'd wish Marcos and Kat had found them first.

"We'll have your wife taken down and moved to our lab. She'll be checked for any clues that may be on her body, and then sent to your choice of funeral homes."

Massito named one of the fanciest in San Diego, and Marcos wrote it down. "Call Detective Cafferty or me if you have any questions," Marcos said.

"By the way," Kat asked, "Who else has a key to the elevator to come up here?"

"No one. We punch in numbers that change each week. We also can see who's at the elevator downstairs. I thought it was an infallible safety system."

Marcos shook his head as he and Kat stepped on the elevator to go down, leaving Massito alone with his grief. "I guess nothing is infallible anymore. There's always going to be someone trying to find the weak spot in the system."

"Unless that person knows all about how to go up and down the elevator," Kat said, as they left the house and walked toward their cars.

"You believe the husband may have killed his wife?"

Kat tipped her head to the side, "I don't know." She straightened. "When he became tearful and spoke of her in such loving terms, I thought I'd made a big mistake. But when he thought we were both looking out the window, I saw a glitter in his eye, almost a smile.

"I'm sure he didn't realize I saw his expression. He's either an excellent actor or he did care for his wife. I'll come back when he's not home and talk with the servants.

"This is going to be an interesting case," Kat said.

"But we must watch our step. If he suspects we don't believe him, he may make us disappear."

"Then you'd better cut out taunting him or causing him to become angry. If he'd kill his wife, the loving husband will have no problem taking care of you."

Kat grinned at her partner. "We'll look out for each other."

* * *

Madison's cell rang, signaling an incoming text as he walked out the door to pick up Karen Kesler. The short message instructed him to report to base, and he knew they had a mission.

He hurried to his car, and his cell rang with an incoming call. He didn't recognize the number, but answered anyway.

"Madison, this is Emma. I know you can't be with us tonight. I'll call Karen and explain you had extra duty come up and that I'll drive her to the meeting. The ladies are interested in her plight and want to help in any way we can. So don't worry. She'll be in good hands."

"I can't thank you enough. I'm certain Karen and her mother-in-law will appreciate any help you can give her and her family. You might check with Cheryl about a good attorney for him that's not too expensive."

"Keep your mind on the mission. We'll handle all the problems back here."

"Thanks." Madison hung up, feeling a great sense of relief.

At the team meeting, Captain Buchanan instructed them on the mission before they boarded the plane to take them to the Middle East. A doctor and nurse had been taken, and their captors were demanding ransom. The SEALs had a short window to rescue them, or they'd be killed.

As usual, Madison checked his medical supplies. Besides being their medic, he spoke several languages. Thankfully, he'd been more involved with that skill than his medic training.

Most of the time, the men weren't hurt. If they did get wounded, he treated them until a plane and other medical staff flew the injured to Germany, which they did quickly.

Once they boarded the plane, Ranger sat beside him. "I guess you'll miss the detective who saved your life."

"She's more interested in getting the bad guys than being involved with me."

"Ah, so you got the cold shoulder."

"No, but I definitely got the message. Detective Cafferty's main interest is her job, not having any involvement with a man."

"Must have been burned bad."

"Yeah, I get the impression the first marriage ended and her heart hardened against all men. Or maybe it's just me."

Ranger leaned back, and they fastened up for take-off. "I hope we'll get back in time for Christmas. We'll definitely miss Thanksgiving two days from now."

"My thoughts were so focused on my parents, I didn't realize how close we were to the holidays."

"Maybe your lady will warm up with all the festivities ahead."

Madison laughed. "I won't hold my breath."

* * *

After they landed and stored their personal articles, they were called to another meeting with Captain Buchanan.

"Our assignment has changed." He frowned and glanced at the team gathered around him. Lowering his voice, he said, "The first team looking for the doctor and nurse somehow lost one of their own men. They need us to locate him while they continue their mission." The Captain laid out a map. "This is the area we'll search. As soon as we find him, we'll join the others. Hopefully, he won't be injured."

"How the hell did he get lost?" Ranger asked.

Captain Buchanan raised his head from the map and frowned. "Lower your voice. Some of the staff here are aligned with the other team. We're not certain, but according to the report, the team member he was assigned to follow sped up without warning. When he looked back, the new SEAL was gone. He hollered, backtracked, but found no evidence of him."

"He'll be blasted for losing his partner," Taylor, better known as Hawke, said.

"Hell, I guess he thought to give this guy a test. It was certainly not the best way to do it."

"What's the SEAL's name?" Madison asked.

"Cory Cafferty, he's twenty-six," the Captain answered.

"Hell, that's weird. Cory's last name is the same as the lady detective's. He must be her brother or some relation," Madison said and ran his fingers through his hair."

"You know him?" Hawke asked.

"His sister is the one who saved my life."

Their Captain straightened. "Okay, team. We owe this family, especially for saving Madison."

They quickly prepared for the search, looked at maps, and headed out to the helo to be dropped near where the SEAL was last seen.

The helicopter landed in a remote field with cover nearby. They jumped out and ran for the trees. Their team leader, Jackson "Bear" Langley, gathered them around and separated the men into two teams.

"Madison and Kijika head east and north, Heath and Hawke, west and south. Ranger, you and I will take the middle. Send word if you find anything," Bear ordered.

The men all nodded. It was almost dark when they turned down their night goggles and moved out.

* * *

Three men surprised Cory and grabbed him. Before he had a chance to fight back, one guy put his hand over Cory's mouth, and the other two carried him far from his SEAL teammate, who had inexplicably sped up and left him behind.

I guess the men were waiting for such an opportunity. Damn, I wonder if I look like a newbie?

When they put him down, he fought all three. He'd grabbed his sidearm when his feet hit the ground. One man reached for it, but Cory shot him and the other one nearby. The third man ran into the bushes.

Cory searched for his partner, but he was well and truly lost. When it started to get dark, he found a small cave near a creek. He pulled scrub up in front of the opening and waited with his gun at the ready.

Not too long afterward, Cory heard voices he recognized as the enemy. He didn't understand the words, but did acknowledge the angry, urgent tone. He barely took a breath. One soldier stopped right beside his small cave. Cory's heart jumped, but he refused to panic. He had a grenade in his belt, but preferred to keep it for later, unless they discovered him.

After what seemed hours, they moved on. Sweat ran down his face and into his eyes, burning them. Still, he didn't move for fear they'd left a guard. He listened to the sounds of the night, a few birds settling down, and the gurgle of the brook. After an hour, he carefully moved his legs and stood, looking out around the brush.

Cory's legs tingled as the blood rushed through them. Since he didn't see or hear anyone, he walked up and down a small area to get the blood flow going. He sat to eat a ration and figure out his next move. He needed a better place to hide, so if he saw men moving toward his hiding spot, he'd recognize whether they were friend or foe.

Glancing around, Cory saw a large, thick tree across

the stream and down about a hundred feet from his position. He moved through the flowing water with his gun held high. They had taken his rifle when he was first grabbed. I'll *make do with my pistol. It's got me this far.*

He chose a spot to exit the stream and walked onto land. He moved through a thicket of brush, making sure he left no trail. Then he decided which was the tallest and thickest tree to climb. He found a spot to settle in and watch for men coming near him, confident he'd be able to see if they were the enemy or rescuers. "I'll be damned if I'm going to die now. I have too much life to live."

The crook in the tree gave him a resting place and cover. He lowered his night goggles and waited to be rescued. He refused to accept any other ending.

* * *

Madison and Kijika headed out. They walked over uneven ground, through thick shrubbery and trees. Kijika motioned Madison to stop. He bent low and put his ear against the ground. "I hear distant footsteps. We need to turn more to the north. According to our map, there's water in that direction. Our SEAL may be walking in a creek so as not to leave any trail.

Madison nodded. "You lead the way."

They walked in single file, Madison keeping an eye out from the rear. It took time to beat or cut some of the dense brush to clear a path. Once Kijika heard what sounded like booted footsteps, and motioned to Madison to hide.

"I see a huge tree with tall bushes," Madison said and led the way. They'd barely ducked for cover before ten men marched by them. A short distance away, the men stopped to make camp.

"Damn," Madison swore in a whisper. He and Kijika moved farther from the camp and found a larger thicket of bushes and trees to hide behind. Bugs flew around them as they quietly dug out an area to lie in. Madison grit his teeth. *I hate bugs. The least favorite part of my job.*

The soldiers made a fire and warmed their provisions. The fragrance had both their stomachs rumbling. They grabbed their food, such as it was, and ate.

As the moon moved across the sky, they settled in and watched the men. Madison whispered, "Do you think we can take them?"

"Maybe. It looks like most are going to sleep and they plan to leave one guard by the fire.

"I think we can take them."

"Wait until no one is stirring. I'll move up and handle the guard," Kijika directed.

As the men settled in for the night and appeared to all be asleep except the guard, Kijika signed he'd check it out. Madison kept his rifle ready.

He watched as Kijika crept silently around the fire, where the guard dozed. As soon as Madison saw the nod and his teammate's knife, he moved forward. They inched around the other sleeping men and killed four before a sound was made.

Two of the men woke up simultaneously and reached for their guns. Madison shot at the firearms and cracked the wood on each one. The others awoke at the sound of gunshots. They looked for their weapons, but Kijika had confiscated them.

"Stay still, or we'll shoot you," Madison said in their language. They stopped moving but glared, with hate in their eyes, at him and Kijika

Madison had radioed their coordinates while he and Kijika were still hiding. When he heard rustling in the forest, he gripped his rifle tighter. A rush of relief swept over him when he saw Bear and Ranger step from between the trees.

Bear grinned. "I guess you two didn't need us after all. Good work. Have you tried to get information from them?" he asked Madison.

"Not yet."

"I'll contact the other teams to head this way. They can guard these guys until the helo gets here." Bear contacted the base to send a helicopter to pick up the prisoners, and the men guarding them.

By dawn, they'd all been carried off. The captured men had their mouths muffled to keep them quiet. Thankfully, only a sliver of the moon cast light during the night.

The transfer completed, the four walked until they found the river, then divided into twos, each going in opposite directions.

Kijika studied the bank as he and Madison moved against the current.

"Bear and Ranger got the easy way," Madison grumbled. "It'll be worth it if we find our SEAL. I don't know how I'd face the lady detective if we don't come back with her brother."

He fell silent and stopped when Kijika put up his hand and pointed to the shore. Then he moved slowly and bent to study the wet ground beside the river and around the bushes. He walked further along the sand and raised his head to study the trees.

CHAPTER 4

Cory heard the men speaking English quietly. *Are these my rescuers, or is this a trick?* As they came closer, he saw two SEALs with black faces. He waited until they were directly below him. The SEAL who looked like an American Indian raised his head and smiled.

"You can come down now. You did a great job protecting yourself until we got here."

Cory moved quickly to reach the ground.

"Be careful," another voice said. "No need to fall and break something now."

When Cory stepped on solid ground, he saluted Kijika and Madison, and said, "Seaman Cory Cafferty."

Once they'd returned his salute and introduced themselves, Madison instructed Cory to move slowly to regain the strength in his legs. "You were in a cramped position for quite a while. You'll most likely feel tingling and maybe cramps in your legs."

"A small price to pay for safety, Sir."

"You did good," Kijika said. "If you keep up the good work, I doubt you'll be a Seaman for long."

"Thank you, Sir."

Madison had just sent the message informing the team of their find when he heard more boot steps. When he saw the enemy moving toward the creek, he quickly notified Bear about their situation. "Damn, I guess this isn't over."

Madison, Kijika and Cory moved back into the denser forest as the soldiers came closer, and then flattened themselves under large bushes.

Madison listened to their conversation and then shifted so he could whisper to Kijika and Cory, "They think the escaped SEAL is still hiding around here. They are going to do another search of the area."

"There must be ten or twelve of them. We're outnumbered," Cory whispered.

"Yes, but I have a plan." Madison quickly drew what he was thinking in the sand. "We must all three get up at once and fire repeatedly," he whispered. Kijika and Cory nodded. He sent a message to Bear and Ranger again, asking for backup.

Madison found a safe spot behind a large tree and several high bushes. He watched as Kijika and Cory found cover nearby. The soldiers searched the side they were on. *Good. It gives Bear and Ranger time to get here.*

One of the enemy soldiers spoke rapidly. Madison quickly signed to Kijika, and he nodded. The soldiers were already walking across the creek. They held their rifles high above the water. Kijika nodded to Madison, and they both fired. Cory shot his gun right after them.

They sprayed bullets all along the creek bed. The soldiers pulled back to get behind trees.

* * *

Cory said a quick prayer and took a deep breath as everyone quit firing for a few minutes. His heart raced and sweat broke out on his forehead, but he took a deep breath and pulled his pistol up to get a good sight for the next attack.

The soldiers regrouped and came out firing. It seemed like bullets flew from all directions. Confused, the soldiers dropped their weapons and gave up as bullets whistled from the front and back, and several of their men fell to the ground.

Kijika, Madison and Cory moved from their hiding places. Madison smiled and said, "It's about time you got here."

"Yeah, your sorry ass would be bullet-ridden if not for us," Ranger said and grinned.

They gathered the guns and tied the prisoners up. One tried to escape while they were talking and got shot in the leg. After that, the rest gave no resistance.

Bear radioed for a helo and let everyone know they had their SEALs all accounted for.

Cory held back. He was embarrassed he'd caused so much trouble by losing sight of his partner walking in front of him. The man they called Bear glanced his way and gave him a hard look.

"Seaman, step forward."

Cory took a deep breath and did as he was told. He

was studied with a stern look as Bear walked around him.

"Are you injured?" Bear asked.

"Only embarrassed and sorry for causing so much trouble."

"Hmmm. Well, you do need to always keep an eye on the man in front of you. But I suspect you've learned that lesson well."

"Yes, Sir."

"Your partner will be disciplined. He knew to notify you to move faster." Bear glanced around and told Madison what to say to their prisoners.

"We've been delayed on looking for our other prisoners, but I expect one of these men will tell us where they're being held. He might get treated much better than his other comrades," Madison said loud enough for the prisoners to hear him.

Then they heard a familiar rhythmic noise and Ranger glanced upward. "Our helo is here."

* * *

Back at the base, it didn't take long for several of the soldiers to give up the position of where the captives were kept, and the number of men holding them.

The other team, already looking for them, returned to base to learn the updated plan to rescue the doctor and nurse. As they were all being given instructions, Ranger leaned close to Madison. "We might get back for Christmas after all."

"Ranger," the Captain snapped his name. "Pay attention."

"Yes, Sir."

The attack was planned for just before dawn. Most of the group holding the prisoners were unofficial combatants who'd abandoned their military. They planned to kill the prisoners at sunrise in two days unless they received the ransom. The SEALs had one day left. Their rescue plan had to work.

Bear looked at Cory. "Captain, I believe Seaman Cafferty has shown himself to be a well-trained SEAL during his first outing. I'd like him to join my team for this assignment."

Captain Buchanan glanced at the young man. "I had planned to let him rest before we flew home. He did well and was under stress."

"Captain, may I speak?" Cory asked.

"Certainly."

"I'd much rather go with the team on this assignment. Every experience I get will make me a better SEAL. I can rest when we all get home."

"Well said. All right, you'll join Bear's team. Be sure you follow instructions."

"I will, Captain."

"Then we all leave at 0500. Get some sleep."

Madison walked back to the barracks with Cory. "When we leave, stay close to me. I owe your sister, and that means making sure you come home."

Cory stiffened and eyed Madison. "Sir, I prefer to be treated like any other SEAL. I want no favors."

Madison laughed. "Good, I had an idea you'd say something like that."

"Another test?"

"Yes, Cory. No more, I promise. You're a good SEAL."

* * *

The men circled the camp where the prisoners were held. "Shadow," Bear whispered Kijika's team name, and he moved slowly to stand by Bear. "Find out where they're being held, which tent."

"Yes, Sir." Shadow moved stealthily through the bushes behind the tents. A guard stood behind the fourth tent on the left side. Shadow watched as he smoked a cigarette, and then crushed it under his foot.

Shadow ducked lower as the guard glanced all around the tent. He seemed satisfied and slid down to the ground to lean against the canvas. When he closed his eyes and appeared to fall asleep, Shadow eased away before contacting Bear.

"Fourth tent from the left. Guard in back, so probably one in front."

"Ok. Most of the men are sitting around the fire. In five minutes, we'll attack from both sides. I'm sending Ranger, Madison, and Cory. Jake will send three of his men. Once we're all in place, the attack will begin. Stay where you are and take out the sleeping, guard, and then rip your way into the tent to protect the hostages. Be quick. Move as soon as we do."

"I will."

Just then, one man sitting with the others around the fire said, "I hope we get the money by noon tomorrow, as we specified."

Bear motioned for Madison to move closer and pointed to his ear.

Madison understood. He lay flat and moved to where he could hear them.

"Doubt it," an older man said. "Will we kill them as we said?"

"No, I have some buyers who'll pay and do it for us. Just to make a splash on the news."

Madison spoke softly in his headset. "They have buyers coming in case they don't get the ransom."

"We're going in," Bear said.

Madison saw the old man put out his cigarette and heard him say, "I'm going to get some sleep."

As the man stood, shots rang out.

* * *

Shadow shot the guard as he tried to stand, and then quickly ripped the back of the tent open with a slash of his knife and stepped inside. A tall, lean man stood in front of a small woman.

"It's all right," Shadow said. "We've come to rescue you.

One of the kidnappers rushed in through the front opening. Shadow shot him and the next who tried to enter. "Get down on the ground, stay close together," he instructed the two.

Shadow opened the front flap and shot at the few

rogue soldiers still trying to keep the rescuers out of their camp. Gradually, the shots lessened, and the SEALs checked each tent. One of them found the older man and tied his hands behind his back. The few left alive dropped their guns.

"You can stand and walk out now," Shadow said to the man and woman huddled on the ground. He held the flap back as they moved into the sunshine. They both put their hands up over their foreheads as the sunlight hurt their eyes.

"We've been in that dark tent for days or weeks. You lose count of time," the doctor said. "I'm Dr. Croft, and this is my assistant, Nurse Willa James. Thank you for rescuing us."

"We're glad we found you," Bear said. "We've called for a helicopter to take you safely out of here."

"You aren't going with us?" Willa asked.

"No. We have some other business to deal with first."

* * *

Once the rescued hostages left, the two teams sat down and planned for their next mission. Bear explained to them, and Captain Buchanan on radio, about the other group headed toward the camp where the doctor and nurse had been held. He explained if no ransom had arrived, the hostages were to be sold to the other group. They would kill them for the publicity.

Captain Buchanan said he'd talk with his superiors and get back to them.

A few minutes later he called back. "We have the okay from higher up."

"You want us to surprise them and bring them in?" Bear asked, to make certain what had been approved.

"Yes. We might as well take care of that group before they find some other Americans to grab," Captain Buchanan said.

"No problem," Bear said, as the other team leader, Jack, nodded.

Afterward, Bear and Jack decided on the method to capture the incoming group of combatants. Jack said his team would circle around and get behind them. "Once we find them, we'll message you."

"Sounds good. We plan to hide in the woods and let them find the empty campsite. They'll be confused at first and think the other group must not have waited for them," Bear said to the two teams. We'll attack at that time."

Once in place, the only sounds were the chirp of birds and the fire crackling as it gradually burned out. They didn't have long to wait.

Bear read the message. Jack's team was following the group. Bear's men were spread out, and he signaled the enemy was near.

This group looked more professional, not as disheveled and unorganized as the first. The man in the lead rode a horse. He pulled the reins back, stopping his mount as he spotted the dying fire and empty camp. He motioned for his men to search the tents.

Bear messaged Jack's group. "Ready?"

"Yes."

The next instant, gunfire filled the air as the men searching the tents dropped to the ground. The head guy on the horse slid off, but Jack slipped behind him and put a gun to his back.

"Don't move, or you'll be dead," Jack ordered. He grabbed the leader's rifle and ordered him to move between the trees. Bear cuffed the leader's hands at his back and pushed him down by a tree. He and Jack wrapped a rope around him and put a gag around his mouth to silence him. When they joined the rest of the men, the last fighters dropped their guns and surrendered. The ones still living were tied up. Bear radioed the helos to take them all back to headquarters.

* * *

Captain Buchanan smiled as they entered the large preparation room. "Good work," he said to his team.

Bear looked around. "Where's Jack and his group?"

"They're getting their equipment together to ship out back home. We're staying a few more days to make certain there aren't any repercussions from today."

Ranger frowned. "What do you mean, we're staying? We completed our assignment."

"We're not certain about these last men. Who are they connected to, and will that person or persons send someone to try and get them out of here? If there is going to be a fight, we need to be here to help."

"Another team can come out and let us go home for Christmas."

Buchanan frowned. "There's no need for another

team. We're here. Accept it. We still might have a chance to get home for the holidays. Ranger, I know this is your first holiday with your wife, but suck it up."

"Yes, Sir. But I don't have to like it."

Buchanan shrugged. "Maybe you should have remained single."

"No, Sir."

"The local government has taken charge and will let us know when they believe it will be safe for us to leave them on their own."

Weary and cranky, the team filed out and went to the barracks. They all found their bunks. Cory stood awkwardly in the center.

"Where are your things?" Bear asked.

"I'm not sure, Sir. I think they may have gone home without me."

"No way. Go check the closet at the end," Hawke said.

Cory grinned when he opened the door and found his bag. "You were right, Sir."

"You can quit calling us 'Sir' here in the barracks," Bear corrected him.

"Thanks, Si… it'll take some getting used to."

* * *

"Any new developments in the death of Camilla Massito?" the Captain asked Kat and Marcos.

"Not much, Sir. Everyone's too afraid of her husband to say anything," Marcos said.

"They haven't been able to find any fingerprints or

information at all from her body or the bedroom. We seem to be at a dead end," the Captain said. "But we can't afford to not find the killer. Every gang in town will feel free to get away with murder. They may not be as smart as Enzo, but they'll try."

"I questioned the servants. They're scared of their boss. They agreed with everything he told us."

"None of them gave any indication they'd talk?"

"No, Captain."

"Go back out. Scout around the grounds. Take some of the lab guys to bring back any unusual items."

"Yes, Sir."

"And stay together. I don't trust the man, but doubt he'd try to make two detectives disappear."

Kat waved at their Captain as they left his office, grabbed their jackets, and headed down to the lab. "Hetty, your favorite forensic tech, might like to go with us," Kat said. "She prefers to be on the scene as often as possible."

They saw Hetty as soon as they entered the lab. She smiled at their request.

"I'd love to go along," Hetty said when asked. "I'll gather some equipment and put on my hiking boots."

"I love those high heels you've got on," Marcos said and added, "they make your legs look sexy."

Hetty blushed and told him to mind his own business. It was usual behavior between the two, but as far as Kat knew, they'd never dated.

They were soon on their way, but were stopped at the Massito gate by a stony-faced guard. After showing their ID, the man stepped inside his booth and called the boss.

"Yes, Sir. They say they want to cover more ground and see the room again. There's a lab lady with them. Yes, I saw her papers. Okay."

After hearing the conversation, Kat was eager to see if Enzo would try to keep them out.

"Boss says you can check the grounds, but not the house until he gets here."

"We'll start on the lawns." Marcos nodded at the guard and drove through the opened gates. "I'll drive along this paved area. Let me know when you two want me to stop."

Kat studied the area out her side of the slow-moving car. Hetty checked out the other side.

"Stop," Hetty ordered.

"What is it?" Kat tried to see out the window beside Marcos.

"The bushes back there." Hetty pointed to the area they'd just passed. "Someone has been taking a short-cut through them."

All three got out of the car and walked to the area. "They're small footsteps, a woman, not a man." Hetty knelt and opened the case she'd brought with her. She measured the footprint and brushed away any loose soil from around the edge of the area to be cast. She looked up at Marcos and Kat. "Might as well go and explore some more areas. This will take me a while. I have what I need in my bag."

"I'm not sure it's safe to leave you alone," Marcos said.

Hetty touched the gun on her hip. "I can take care of myself."

"Maybe."

"You stay here, Marcos," Kat said, ending the argument. "I see a woman nearby cleaning the veranda. I'm going to casually drive partway there and then walk up and talk to her."

Marcos stood by Hetty and nodded. "Fire your gun if you want me to join you."

Kat laughed. "I'm sure the neighbors would appreciate hearing a gunshot almost as much as I'd appreciate filling out the paperwork for firing my weapon." She got in the car and drove along the road where she turned toward the veranda, parked, and hid behind some bushes.

The woman hadn't noticed Kat. Kat crept closer. She moved onto the walkway, not far from the area being cleaned.

The woman jumped when Kat came up behind her and touched her arm. "Sorry to frighten you," Kat said with an apologetic smile. "You didn't hear me call out with your machine on."

She was a small, dark-skinned woman somewhere around forty or fifty. "What are you doing here?" she asked, her words tinged with a slight Spanish accent.

Kat showed her badge. "I'm doing a little more checking. I don't remember seeing you when I talked with the other servants right after Mrs. Massito died."

"No, I was sick."

"Oh, I'm sorry to hear that. Can we talk now? Perhaps you could stop working and sit a minute."

"I get in trouble if not working."

"No, you won't. I'll explain to Mr. Massito."

She made a sound of disbelief. "Mr. Massito does not listen, even to a lovely wife."

"Did they get along?"

The servant glanced around and then whispered, "When she did exactly what he said."

"Was she happy?"

"Only pretended when they were with others." She leaned forward and her voice lowered even more. "She hated and feared him. He laughed when he saw her fear."

Suddenly, she drew back from Kat. "Go. Boss man car just came through the gate. He mustn't see me talking to you."

"I can keep you safe."

She gave a sarcastic laugh. "Like the other cop promised Miss Camilla?" The maid grabbed her cleaning supplies and went inside.

Kat walked to the unmarked car and watched as Enzo's vehicle stopped beside where Hetty and Marcos were working. She quickly got in and drove in their direction. She saw Enzo Massito get out of his expensive-looking vehicle and stalk towards her colleagues, his mouth moving.

Enzo turned as Kat got out of the car and walked over to join them. Massito turned on her. "And where have you been?"

"I drove around, but didn't find any other clues."

"So you still have no evidence as to who killed my wife?"

"No luck so far, but we aren't giving up."

"Well, finish up and get off my property."

"We found a footprint. It's probably nothing, but we have to check it out, and let this cast dry before we take it in," Marcos said.

"Hurry up," he snarled. His face turned an ugly shade of red as he glared at all three.

"You need to calm down," Kat said. "I'd bet you're close to having a stroke."

He threw her a nasty look and stomped off to his car. Then he spun the tires as he drove away.

"An edgy, angry suspect. I wonder what or who made him mad," Hetty said as she straightened.

Kat got on her phone to the Captain. She explained where they were and what had happened. "Can we have two uniforms to guard this footprint? I'd like to do a raid on his home this evening about midnight. He's riled up, Captain, and doesn't want us around. I think something has him worried."

"All right, if I can get a Judge to agree. We have very little evidence other than he's the only one who knew how to use the elevator. This better help us find good evidence to get this guy if he did do his own wife in."

The others had heard her side of the conversation. "Hetty, when the uniforms get here, you can leave and come back in the morning to get the cast."

"Thanks, I dreaded sitting out here alone for even a few hours. And if there's a mist or anything it'll take longer to dry."

Kat glanced at Marcos. "We're doing a raid at midnight."

"Great. Enzo may have gotten lax, and we'll find something that'll let us take him in for more questioning. As soon as the uniforms get here, I'll leave. I need a few hours of sleep before the raid. What about you, Kat?"

"No, I'm too keyed up. I'll go to the station and make notes about what we did and found today."

"Go ahead. We'll wait for the uniforms," Marcos said and nodded to Hetty. "We can sit and talk while we wait, and then I'll call my buddy to pick us up."

"Then I'm headed out. See you at midnight."

CHAPTER 5

Kat passed up doing paperwork and stopped by her parents' house. She'd get a meal, then go home and sleep a few hours.

"Hi, Mom." Kat leaned across her mother to smell the stew she was stirring on the stove. "It smells great and looks done." Then she looked closer at her mother's expression. "What's up?"

"I haven't heard from Cory. The last time he called, he didn't have much to say." Kat's Mom put her hand on her heart. "Something is wrong. I feel it here," she said, patting her chest. Tears came into her eyes.

Kat took the spoon from her mother's hand and placed it on the counter. Then she walked her Mom to the nearest chair and bent to look her in the eyes.

"Cory warned you there were times when he couldn't call. I'm certain he will contact you the first chance he gets."

Tears streamed down her mother's face. "I know..."

she took a deep breath and straightened her posture. "I suppose I'll get used to this job of his."

"We all have dangerous jobs, Mom."

"But you and the others are here. I'd know right away if you needed me."

"Last I talked to Cory, he sounded happy, Mom. Don't let him see how much this bothers you. He might give up the job he's dreamed of doing, and he worked hard to get accepted."

"If only he'd never met that SEAL instructor who told him about the job and encouraged him to try out for the position." Kat's Mom looked up at her. "I never thought he'd get through all the rigorous training."

"You have to be proud, Mom. Many don't succeed. Cory had no problems doing whatever they threw at him."

Her Mom took a deep breath. "You're right." She glanced at the clock. "What are you doing here on a weekday?"

"I was hungry, and I need to eat and sleep for a few hours. I'm on call," she said rather than tell her mother exactly what she'd be doing.

"Oh, dear. That's dangerous, too. I should have married another teacher. Maybe all my children would have become teachers or something else safe."

"You know you love Dad bunches. You've told us all these years how you met and couldn't resist his Irish charm."

Her father peeked his head around the doorway. "Is someone talking about me?" he asked with a grin.

"We won't tell you. You'll get a big head," Kat teased.

He walked into the kitchen. "Good to see you, Kat. We don't usually get a visit during the week."

"She's going on a raid at midnight."

"Ah, Momma," her father said and kissed her. "You worry too much about our children. They can handle themselves."

"I know, I know. I just wish our youngest would call." As though summoned by magic, the phone rang. Kat's mother grabbed it. She visibly sagged as she saw the number on the display. "Thank goodness. I'm so happy to hear your voice, Cory."

Kat glanced at her father. "She knows all our numbers."

He grinned, "Let's get a bowl of stew and let her be."

Fifteen minutes later, red-eyed, but smiling, Kat's mother joined them with her own bowl of stew.

"You've been crying again," her husband noted in a soft tone. "Is Cory all right?"

"For now." She told them about his capture and all that happened. "He says he's fine. I'll believe it when he gets home and I see for myself."

"When will that be?" Kat asked.

"They leave tonight for San Diego. He'll have time off and plans to come to dinner on Sunday. He said he's bringing a friend, a SEAL, one of the ones who saved his life." She wiped the tears away with the corner of her apron. "I knew in my heart he was in danger."

"But now you know he's okay," Kat's Dad said.

She took a deep breath. "Yes, but I won't believe Cory's uninjured until I see it with my own eyes."

"Sunday's not far away, Mom. You'll see him soon."

* * *

When Madison told Cory about how his sister had saved his life, the younger man laughed. "That's my sister. She's good at her job."

"I'm glad she was in the right place and at the right time for me."

"I told Mom I planned to bring you to Sunday dinner when I called. She'll be glad to meet one of the SEALs who saved me."

"You did a lot to keep yourself safe. But I'll be glad to meet your family and see your sister again."

"Be careful. If you're interested in Kat, she's held everyone at bay since her divorce. I doubt she'd risk falling for a SEAL who's gone from home so much."

"Don't worry. I'd like to be friends, that's all. I'm divorced, and I understand her caution."

"How long have you been divorced? She's going on five years."

"A year of separation and about the same since the divorce. I tend to like my own company. I'm not much of a people person except at work."

"It sounded like you were just describing Kat. You two may work out fine."

Madison pretended he would punch Cory. "Don't be matchmaking."

Cory laughed and moved out of range. "I think you protest too much."

* * *

Enzo Massito showed his anger as he stood with his bodyguard reading the paper that gave the police the right to check his house and belongings. He frowned at Kat and Marcos.

"I told you, I loved my wife. You and your police can't find the right person, and you're trying to put the blame on me. Stand right there while I call my attorney."

He moved away from them to make a call from his cell. They couldn't hear what he was saying, but his expression told Kat the conversation wasn't going the way he wanted it to.

"Apparently, his attorney is telling him we have the right to do a search," Kat said. "His face is so red I fear he might have a stroke."

Massito flung the phone across the room. "I will not forget this," he snarled at Kat and Marcos. He and his goon stepped back, allowing them to enter.

At least eight officers and uniforms rushed in, all going in different directions. "Give me the key to your elevator, please," Kat said and held her hand out.

"Watch your step," Massito warned her. "It may take time, but you will come to regret this."

Kat glanced around and called one of the uniforms over. "He threatened me. Take him to jail."

Massito sputtered. "What the *fuck*. I was angry. Can't a man be angry in his own house?"

"Not when it's you, and you make a threat. Take Mr. Massito to the jail," she directed the uniform.

When he walked out of sight, Marcos leaned close.

"He's a dangerous enemy. His tentacles reach far. Be very careful."

"We can't let him be belligerent to us and make threats. He'll only make more."

"Let's see if we can find enough evidence to keep him in jail," Marcos said.

Once Kat got the key for the elevator, she and Marcos went upstairs. "I'll start with her closet. You go through his."

Kat was awed by the large room called a closet. "It's big enough to be another bedroom," she called out to her partner.

"His is fairly big, but not as much as you're implying." Marcos walked to the other end of the bedroom and came in to see what Kat was talking about.

"Wow. If I ever get married, I don't want my wife to see a room like this one."

"I know what you mean. Women would fight for this type of closet. I wonder if Mrs. Massito was happy in here or it was a private place to cry?"

"Hell, most women would love all she had."

"No. I think Massito's wife lived in fear most days and would have loved a little cabin in the woods all alone. I feel sadness in this room. Don't you?"

"I'll leave all those weird feelings to you ladies. I'm going back to his closet, not nearly as big or as fancy."

Kat wandered around the room. It was spooky, but she felt the sadness, the longing to be free. *I'd better go through all these shoeboxes and dresses before it gets too late.*

She'd almost finished when she backed out of a row of gowns and hit her foot on a large, fancy box that reached Kat's waist. She opened it and realized it was the hamper. *Damn big basket.* Tipping it over, she pulled out the few dirty clothes inside. Then she noticed a tiny piece of silk. She pulled on it, and the bottom of the basket moved up to reveal a narrow space.

"Ah, so you did rebel and have a place to hide things."

Inside the opening was a small, thin tablet of paper. Kat sat on the floor and opened it. There were several pages detailing how much Camilla Massito hated her husband and her life.

He'll kill me soon. He loves telling me he's found my replacement and hasn't decided my fate. I hope that Jeff can help me escape before I die. But can I trust him? Maybe he's a plant from Enzo.

The worst day of my life was when I reluctantly agreed to decorate Enzo's house. When he insisted I marry him, I agreed. What choice did I have? He might look for a reason and discover my real family.

"More mystery and no answers." Kat stood as Marcos came into the closet. She held up her find. "We'll take the tablet and have this room torn apart by our forensic people. This is new information I literally stumbled upon, and there may be a few more things we've missed."

She handed the tablet to Marcos. "You might want to read this before we leave."

Kat made a call for forensics to check the upstairs level and the elevator. Then she and Marcos walked toward the elevator to return to the main floor.

"Wait," she said. "Look to the left, in the corner. Do you see something shiny?"

"I do now. When you shut off the light behind us, it glowed."

"What's behind that wall?"

"No idea. How can we get to it?" Marcos knocked on the wall around where they'd both seen something.

"It's hollow."

"Yes." Marcos took out his phone and called their supervisor to relay what they'd found. "Can we knock part of the wall out to see what it is?"

"I'll talk to the chief and see what he says. Hold on."

To Kat, it seemed like hours before the supervisor came back on the line. "He's going to send a man over who can get whatever it is with the least damage. He'll be about twenty minutes. Meanwhile, lock up the elevator. We don't want to be disturbed by one of Enzo's goons."

"I've always suspected Enzo had another way to come up to these rooms. We'll look for it as we wait," Marcos said.

"You don't have to look for it," Massito said from behind them. "I'll show you before I have my men take you away and dispose of the bodies."

Massito's eyes shone with such evil Kat barely kept from shivering. "How did you get out of jail?"

He faced her and laughed. "Several judges are friends. I had one called, and he ordered my release immediately for lack of evidence. You almost fell for my story. But I'm the cleverest one of the three of us. I knew you'd decide it had to be me. I've had eyes on you for some time.

"Good for you for finding Camilla's tablet. She hid it

well. I no longer needed her when I found someone much happier to please me.

"She was right, you know. I sent a man to pretend an interest in her. She believed in his kindness and promise to help her get away." He sighed. "Then the fool actually fell for her and truly planned her rescue. It's his footprint you found. A nice young man. Too bad he preferred my wife to loyalty to me."

He looked Kat up and down. "I think having you before I send you away to be killed might be fun."

Massito moved closer and ran his finger along the edge of her jaw. Kat moved quickly and bit his finger. He hit the side of her face with his gun and she fell at his feet.

"I'd like to kill you now, but first I'll sexually enjoy you and your partner will watch." He turned to Marcos. "Take the ties from the curtains and put them on the bed. Then undress her. This will be so much fun."

Evilness has a smell, Kat thought. It oozed out of a person's pores when excited. She'd smelled it several times before, but Massito's odor was stronger. When Marcos leaned down to put her on the bed, she whispered, "Gun. Ankle."

Massito moved closer. "What did she say?"

"That she hopes to see you dead."

He laughed and moved his gun along her jawline. "When I am through with you, I'll take pleasure in killing both of you. But your friend here will die fast. I intend to watch you suffer as I shoot you many times in many places."

"The cops are downstairs. They'll hear your gun."

"No. I often beat my wife with none the wiser. This room is soundproof and no one heard. Of course, I was careful to hit her in places that wouldn't show."

"You're a monster and will die either being taken into custody or when you're found guilty of murder. I plan to be in the courtroom to watch your verdict handed down."

He slapped her and grabbed her neck. "I'll kill you now, you bitch."

In his anger, he'd forgotten Marcos. Marcos grabbed a heavy vase from a side table and hit him in the head. When Massito's hand lowered his gun for a second, Kat grabbed hold and fought for it. The gun went off. Massito gaped at her, then they both looked down at his chest and the bullet hole that darkened his shirt. His eyes closed and he went limp. She pushed him off her and knelt over him.

While Marcos called for an ambulance, Kat whispered in Massito's ear. "I want you to live, and I'll see you and all your men go to trial. I don't know whether I want you to die or live a long life in prison."

She looked down at his blood all over her body. "I need to shower and clean up, but first unlock the elevator so the police can move in and check the scene as it is." She swung a sheet around her enough to not be fully naked.

Police hurried out of the elevator and looked around the room.

"Is he dead?" one of the officers asked.

"No. We've called for an ambulance. The EMTs will arrive soon."

Seeing the blood, an officer asked, Are you shot Detective Cafferty?"

"No, he tried and we fought for the gun. It's his blood on me. Can you take a sample and pictures as needed so I can shower?"

"We might need a sample of blood for evidence." The officer motioned the lab tech forward. "Get what you need so she can get clean."

Marcos pulled out a small recorder. "I managed to turn it on when he focused his attention on her. He apparently likes to beat up on women."

"Give the recorder to me."

"I will once we have a copy."

"We are allowed to have it now."

"I might have to shoot you if you try and take it from me. We're the detectives on the case and I plan to copy it first. This is our crime scene."

* * *

When Kat finally got to shower, bruises were showing up on her skin as the soap and water cleaned her. Her whole body hurt, especially her throat where Massito tightened his hand on her neck. She finished showering off and rubbed dry with a warm, fluffy towel.

It took a while to find a loose summer dress that fit her and panties that were tight. Wearing them was uncomfortable, but better than facing all the men in the other room with nothing on but a dress. *They might not know, but I will.* I felt terribly naked wrapped in the sheet.

The EMTs were working on Massito as she walked out of the dressing room. Once he was intubated and medicated, the EMTs rushed for the elevator and hurried downstairs. As soon as she saw Scott, she raced into his arms and cried.

"It's okay. I'm here. No one else is going to hurt you."

"I know, but I can't stop shaking." He grabbed the comforter which had been thrown off the bed and wrapped her in it. Then Scott picked her up and headed for the elevator, which had returned full of forensic staff to go over the room.

Kat tried to talk, but her voice was too hoarse. She pointed to the wall.

"Don't worry," Marcos said. "I'll show them."

* * *

Cory got a message as they were disembarking at the base. Stunned, he stopped on the plane's steps.

"Move ahead," someone hollered.

"Sorry." Cory rushed down the last few steps to the tarmac.

Madison, who was right behind him, touched his arm. "Bad news?"

Cory took a deep breath. "My sister, Kat, has been hurt and is being taken to the hospital. I'm to meet my parents in the emergency room."

"I'll drive you," Madison said and pointed to his car. "We'll come back for your vehicle after we see your sister."

"Thanks, but there's no need for you to drive me, Sir. I'm okay."

"Maybe, but you look more upset than you did when facing the bad guys."

"There are six of us and only two sisters. We've always been protective of them. None of us liked the idea when Kat decided to become a police officer and now a detective." He looked up at Madison. "I guess that makes us a bit chauvinistic."

"No, I think it indicates a loving family who are concerned about each other." As they got in the car, Madison asked, "How did your parents take your desire to be a SEAL?"

"Pretty good, but Mom worries a lot."

"I think all our Moms do. I insist you let me drive you to the hospital. Where is she?"

When he named the one in town, Madison nodded. "I know the fastest way to get there. It's the same one they took me to when I was hurt."

As they headed to town, Cory grinned. "I think you're a bit sweet on my sister."

"If I was, I'd never tell you. I've only been single for a couple of years. I tend to like alone time and not a lot of partying."

"Ah, you sound much like Kat."

Madison frowned. "Don't start expecting anything between your sister and me. I don't think she even likes me much." *But I'd like to find the man who hurt her.*

While they were en route, Cory got another message from his mother that Kat had been admitted and sent up to the third floor, Room 366.

After Madison parked, they rushed to the nearest elevator. They got out on the third floor and Cory rushed over to a tall, lovely older woman. He immediately pulled her into his arms for a hug.

"How's Kat?" Cory asked.

"Better. I think it's more emotional than physical, although Kat is covered in bruises." Cory's Mom looked around him at Madison.

"Sorry, I didn't introduce you first, Mom. This is Chief Petty Officer, Madison Carney. He's one of the men who rescued me."

Madison put out his hand, but Mrs. Cafferty pulled him into a hug. "You saved my boy's life. I can never thank you enough."

Blushing, Madison said, "It wasn't only me, Mrs. Cafferty. Our whole team was involved." He smiled and added, "Your daughter saved me not long ago from a man pointing a gun in my direction."

"Ah, what a coincidence. You must both come in and say hello to Kat. She's a bit calmer, and it may help her to see the two of you."

"Kat's been upset, Mom? I've never seen her lose her cool."

"She had a bad experience. Apparently, the man threatened to rape her and then kill her with her partner watching. I've never seen her this way."

"Maybe I ought to stay outside. Your daughter might prefer to have only family members see her in this shape." Madison tightened his hands into fists. *He'd like to get his hands on whoever hurt her.*

"You have a quiet and calm about you, Madison.

We've been so upset. Kat may need one person who isn't crying over her."

Madison took a deep breath. "I'd rather you ask her if she's okay with it, first."

Mrs. Cafferty smiled and nodded. "I will. I like you. You must come to our Sunday dinner so all the family can thank you for your part in bringing Cory home." She smiled at her son. "He's my baby, and I worry about him."

"I understand. I'm an only child. My Mom does the same."

"Come on, Cory. Kat is waiting to see you."

Madison strolled down the hall and found a chair facing a window. *I must prepare myself to see her and not show the emotion racing through my body. Damn, any man who abuses a woman, and....* He reluctantly admitted, *especially not one I may care about more than I want too.*

Mrs. Cafferty found him about ten minutes later. "She wants to see you."

"Are you sure you didn't convince her?" he asked with a smile.

"Perhaps a bit, but not much. Kat's very pleased you helped find Cory. Come, don't be bashful."

Madison laughed. "I don't think anyone has called me bashful since kindergarten." He walked beside Mrs. Cafferty to the door to Kat's room.

"Go on inside. I'll wait out here. I think there may be something Kat needs to ask you. Cory will join me when you go in."

The shades on the window were down partway,

leaving Kat in a shadow where she lay in the bed. Cory nodded to him as he walked out.

"I hope I'm not disturbing you," Madison said.

"No, I've had visitors all night and morning. I'm tired, but my brother shared some of what he went through during his mission. Thank you for bringing him home, you and all of your team."

"We never leave a team member behind."

"Thank goodness. I don't know what my family would do without our baby brother. It's difficult to see him as a SEAL."

"He's already excellent. He kept himself alive until we got there."

"We were all worried about him."

"Did they have questions about you being a detective?"

She tried to smile and winced. "That hurt. Many questions. I had to fight them all."

"Why was it so important, this job, this particular career?"

"I grew up hearing stories from my Dad, who is a retired Police Chief, and my brother, who's a Detective. It's all I ever wanted to be."

Madison studied her bruised face and neck, and what he could see of her arms. He suspected there were more injuries under her sheet. "It's a dangerous job."

She tried to smile, but it obviously hurt. "So is your job."

"But we have no women SEALs."

"True. Maybe I should try out."

He couldn't help but laugh. "I've heard some women

have tried, but they couldn't get through all you have to withstand to be called a SEAL. In the future, a woman will come along who surprises us all."

"Damn right."

Shaking his head, Madison asked, "Is your job worth what you went through last night?"

Kat closed her eyes for a second. "I think so."

"You don't sound too sure."

Through tight lips, she spoke in a low voice, "The man we were after threatened to rape me and shoot me in many places before I died."

Madison clenched his teeth, and his hands tightened into fists. "Where the hell was your partner?"

"He was there. He helped free me."

"But I heard you shot the guy."

"Yes, and I hope he lives to go to jail." She shivered, and a frightened expression crossed her face. Through chattering teeth, she said, "I... cannot stop all this shaking."

Madison slipped out of his shoes and put the bed rail down. Then he lay beside her and wrapped his warm body around her. "It's all right," he whispered. "You're still in shock. It will wear off."

"I'm so cold."

"I'll pull this blanket up over us."

Gradually, her shaking subsided, and her eyes closed. Her breathing told Madison she was sleeping.

Mrs. Cafferty peeked into the room. She studied the two entwined on the bed, nodded and smiled. Quietly, she walked out and closed the door.

CHAPTER 6

When Kat woke, she felt warm and safe. She blinked her eyes and turned her head to see Madison Carney was wrapped around her. A slight smile came to her face. *He must be tired.* Then she remembered his gentle questioning and his caring expression.

I remember wanting to see him. Feeling only he might understand what happened and my response. But why? There's an attraction between us, but I don't understand this feeling of trust. Usually it takes much more time for a person to gain my confidence, especially a man.

Suddenly, his eyes opened and he smiled. "I think your intense thinking woke me up."

"Probably me staring at you. You are a strange man. I don't understand why I needed you to calm me. My mother and brothers ought to have been able to help me. They tried, but the shaking kept coming back."

"I think you knew I'd understand because I've been where I had to use my own skills to save myself. It's never a comfortable situation, and it changes us in a way others wouldn't grasp."

"Exactly. I'm so happy you realize what I'm feeling. I love my family, but they kept saying, 'See now, you have to change jobs.' I doubt if my brother had been in a similar situation, he'd have been given the same advice."

"I've never been in a large family situation, but I expect they may say the same to whoever got hurt. The family members I've met seem protective and involved."

"What about your parents?"

He chuckled. "If they knew half of what my job entailed, they'd be trying to find me a nice girl to marry and have me come home to live."

"What got you into the SEALs?"

"I was teaching history at the local college and taking a course to be a medic. That was during my second year of teaching. I also went to the gym most nights after work. It turned out the father of one of my student's saw me there. We talked, and I found out he was home on vacation. He was a Navy SEAL."

"I asked him about the job, and he told me as much as he could. He'd come to see his son. His wife hadn't handled the many times he had to be away very well. She moved back here to be near her parents, and they divorced. We met at the gym most nights while he was there. The last night he suggested I come to San Diego, meet his team, and consider trying out."

"So, you did."

"Yes, I grew more and more certain it was the job for me. The next year I moved to San Diego, joined the

Navy, and asked to try out for the SEALs. The SEAL I'd met gave me a strong recommendation."

"And you didn't want to let him down. I gather you got through on the first try."

"Yes, and I love my job, doing good for my country."

"That's why you understand how I feel."

"Perhaps, but I think your father and brother working in the police force had an influence on you. Also, with so many brothers, I expect you felt you needed to show them what you can do."

"Perhaps some, but that didn't affect my whole decision."

"Think about it and tell me what else helped make your decision."

She stared hard at him. "You are like the rest of my family and think I ought to resign my position."

He shook his head. "No. I want you to consider what you really want to do with your life."

"Be a police lieutenant."

"I meant for you to give it more thought instead of a snap decision." Madison moved off the bed and buttoned and tucked in his shirt. At one-point last night, she'd got his shirt open and slept against his warm chest. When he glanced at her, she was blushing.

"Did I do that?"

"Yes, but no problem."

"Still, I am sorry. Whatever came over me, I don't fully understand." Kat shook her head.

"No problem. I wanted to warm you up. You were cold and shaking."

She closed her eyes and clenched her fist around the

sheet. *It's so confusing. What is there between this man and me?*

His fingers rubbed along the place on her forehead where she frowned. "Whatever is worrying or confusing will become clear eventually. After such an incident, there has to be some coming to terms with it."

Her hand reached out when he turned to go. "Do you have to leave?"

"For now. I'll be back. But if you need me sooner," and have forgotten my number…" He handed her a card with his name and phone number. "I've got to call my folks and let them know I'm home and well. My Dad mustn't be worrying too much."

Kat blushed. "I'm sorry I kept you so long."

He took quick steps to her side. "I'm glad I helped. Don't hesitate to call." He bent down, kissed her lightly on the mouth and hurried out of her room.

* * *

Madison drove slowly home. *I'm tired, and I don't want a speeding ticket. What I want is some much-needed sleep before thinking about my reactions to my Amazon detective.* Madison smiled when he thought about the nickname he'd given her. *I'll phone my parents and then collapse on my bed.*

"Hi!" his Mom said as soon as she answered the phone. "We were worried. You'd said you were on your way home."

"Sorry, the lady detective who saved my life was in

the hospital. I drove her brother to see her and then stayed longer than expected."

"Your Dad said you were most likely involved in helping someone and for me not to worry. You are all right? No injuries?"

"No, Mom. I'm fine. As I told you, I was helping the lady who shot my attacker. I called and notified you of that event."

"Are you completely well?" she asked.

"Completely. Don't worry."

He heard the smile in her voice as she promised, "I will try not to worry. Here's your Dad."

"Hi, son. How's it going?"

"Fine for me. How about you?"

"You know your Mom. She's smothering me with love and directions to eat and rest. I had my physician tell her to back off and not be so anxious."

Madison chuckled. "Did she listen?"

"Not much, but it's a bit better. Your Mom is a sweetheart, and I don't want her to change too much."

"I hope I can find a wife who'll love me that way."

"You will. Don't rush. Are you coming home for Christmas? Thanksgiving's already gone by."

"I doubt it, Dad. I had quite a bit of time off already. I think I'll work most of the holiday so my teammates can be with their families."

"It's the right thing to do. If my doctor says okay, we'll fly there and spend a few days with you."

"Sounds good. Let me know if you can come. I hate to cut this short, but I'm falling asleep standing up."

"Get your rest. We'll talk another time. Love you, son."

"Same here, Dad." Madison went into the kitchen and drank two glasses of water, then dropped his clothes as he walked to the bedroom and fell asleep on his covers.

When Madison woke, it was dark outside. He blinked, surprised to see the clock showing eight o'clock at night. *I feel like if I laid back down, I'd sleep another eight hours, but I want to check on Kat.*

Forcing himself to get up, he walked into the bathroom and turned the shower on to cold. He groaned when he got in, but it woke him up.

He came out of the bathroom with a towel wrapped around his hips and the sound of his cell phone ringing.

"Hello?"

"Madison, this is Cory."

"What's up?"

"I thought you'd want to know. Two men broke into my sister's room and took her. They pushed Mom around, but didn't shoot her, thank goodness. They shot a nurse who tried to intervene. They say she'll live. We must rescue Kat. Will you help?"

"Let me run this by the Captain. Maybe I can get several of our team to join us. Either way, I'll be there soon."

"Thanks."

"Damn, damn, damn. I should have stayed with her." He quickly called Captain Buchanan and explained the problem.

"As long as the men going with you are not on duty,

I don't see a problem with them helping. Keep me informed and try not to get shot."

"Yes, Sir."

Madison's next call was to Ranger. Tersely, he filled his friend in. "Can you help?"

"Sure, and Kijika's here with me. We'll head your way."

"I'll let Cory know who's joining him at the hospital. We'll hopefully pick up the trail from there."

Madison paced the floor while he waited. He'd gathered the equipment they might need and his medical case. Once his teammates arrived, they decided to all ride in Ranger's truck.

"Do we have any idea where they may have taken her?" Ranger asked.

"No, not a clue. I hope they left something behind to help us," Madison said. "And I'm happy they didn't shoot Mrs. Cafferty, but I think they knew that would rile up every police department and sheriff's department in San Diego County and beyond. From what I've gathered, the Caffertys are well known and well thought of in this area."

Ranger swung into the closest parking spot, and they got out and marched into the hospital. A security officer stopped them. "We need to see your credentials," he said and touched the gun by his side.

"We're friends of Cory Cafferty," Madison said as he pulled out his wallet to show his Navy ID.

The guard swallowed and cleared his throat, realizing the three big men standing in front of him were most likely SEALs. "Go right on up to the third floor. I'll let them know to let you by."

"Thanks," Ranger said as they put their IDs away and rushed to the elevators.

The door opened on the third floor, and another security guard walked with them to Kat's room. Her mother sat in a chair with her husband and son, Cory, close by.

Madison knelt in front of Mrs. Cafferty. "Are you all right?"

"Yes," she whispered. "A few bruises is all. I'm so worried about what they'll do to Kathleen."

"Hi, Cory," Madison said as he looked at the other man.

Cory came to his side and introduced his father and the tall man beside them as his brother, Scott, also a police detective. Then Madison introduced the other SEALs.

"We never thought of anyone kidnapping her in the hospital," her father explained. "She was to go home with us today."

"I wonder if the kidnappers had that information," Madison commented.

"Not unless someone on this floor is working for Enzo Massito," Scott said.

"Did he get out?"

"No. We have him under close watch and have had since he was arrested, but he may have made plans for her before his arrest and told his men what to do. I'm sure someone in his organization is responsible," Scott said. "I think you may be right. They most likely planned for such a situation."

"I'd just woken up and showered when I got the call. If I hadn't been so tired, I'd never have left your sister alone. At least I ought to have seen she had someone with her for protection."

"We don't need anyone else blaming themselves," Ranger said. "Let's make a plan. How about I go downstairs and talk to the people who take care of the entrance in the front and side."

"Good idea." To Kat's father, Madison said, "Mr. Cafferty, I think you might have your wife checked in the emergency room, and then take her home. We'll keep in close touch with you."

"She said she's getting a headache. I'll have her checked."

"I've already asked the nurses to call each floor and see if any patient or staff saw anything unusual out their windows this morning," Cory added.

"Excellent idea." Madison glanced around the room. "Does anyone have an idea where we might start looking for Kat?"

"I gave Kat a necklace for Christmas last year," Scott said. She loves cats, but she's allergic to them. As I expected, she wears it all the time. What she doesn't know is that inside the cat is a small tracker. I always worried she'd get in a tight spot and need me. But I tried to contact it, but there was no response."

"Kijika, will you check the outside of the hospital?"

"Sure."

"Especially look for her necklace. They may have

pulled it off her in the struggle to get her in their car. I doubt she went quietly."

Cory shrugged. "She's never done anything quietly since she was born, or so I've heard."

Madison turned back to Scott. "Can you give me the information on how to track someone wearing her particular necklace? I've got a friend who is better than anyone I know at finding people. He might be able to pick up the signal where an ordinary computer wouldn't be strong enough."

"Sure, I have them in my pocket." Scott pulled out a sheet of information. "This came with it."

"Excuse me. I'll try to contact my friend and have him start searching for your sister." Madison pulled out his phone and strode out of the room, quickly locating a quiet corner on the third floor to make his call. He dialed Tex number.

"Hi, Madison. I was glad to hear you were back."

Madison explained the situation. "I'm going to see if the nurses will let me send this to you with their fax machine, and I'll also take a picture of the paper and text it to you. It's been folded and is very wrinkled so the fax copy might be better. I'd like to have you looking for her as soon as possible. I think her life will depend on us finding her quickly."

"I'll get right on it."

Madison laid out the paper, took and picture and faxed it to Tex. Then he looked for the Head Nurse. One of the nurses at the desk paged her, and she soon came out of a patient's room, walking briskly toward the nurse's station. A nurse standing at the counter explained Madison's request to use their fax machine.

"Certainly, come into my office. My machine is a bit newer and faster."

He followed her in, and she quickly inserted the instructions and sent them to Tex.

"I hope this helps. I'm so sorry these men managed to take her away from here."

"I understood one of your nurses was injured trying to stop them."

"Yes, but she'll be fine. She ducked at the right time, and the bullet only grazed her arm. Do you think you can find our patient?"

"I'm determined we will. The man I sent the paperwork to is the best I know at tracking people."

"Good."

He waved his thanks and stepped out of her office.

"Ranger call all the floors and see if anyone saw, heard, or found anything. Kijika's out in the parking lot, searching the grounds. The kidnappers may have dropped something, especially her necklace. Ranger, when you finish calling all the floors and Kijika returns, we'll search Massito's house. Cory mentioned it when we were driving here. I'll ask Scott about a warrant."

"You think they'd go there?"

"They might. Cory said he'd driven by there once or twice on the way out of town and that it was huge."

"All right by me. At least we'll be doing something."

Scott and Cory joined them. "We want to be included," Scott said.

"When we get there, we'll search the woods around

the house," Scott said. "My gut tells me Massito liked to have all his business nearby."

When they'd all left the room, Madison sat in a nearby chair and put his head against the wall. He closed his eyes and remembered the fear he'd seen in Kat's eyes before he left. *If only I'd waited.* "Damn," he muttered.

"Here's a cup of coffee," a soft voice said.

He opened his eyes to see a nurse sitting down beside him. Madison noticed she had a white bandage on her arm.

"I have information, but I didn't want to share it with just anyone. I can see your real concern for our patient." She wrung her hands and didn't look at him.

Not wanting to scare her away, Madison let her build up the courage to speak.

"I used to date this cute guy. I thought he was the one. No man had treated me so politely or seemed to care for me that much. But one day, I came home, and he was gone. A week later, he called and said he was on a new job, and he wouldn't be seeing me again."

"How did you learn that the man you dated was someone else?"

"I saw a picture of him standing by a tough guy I knew was the head of a gang. Everyone knew the police had tried to get something on this gangster over the years, but he was too clever. I heard he'd married someone." Tears came into her eyes. "And recently read about his wife's death."

"You knew her?"

"She was my sister. I never got to speak with her

after her marriage to him. Whenever I saw her away from the mansion, she was with at least two of his men. I was a coward. Maybe if I'd gone to the police...."

"He'd have had her say she married him willingly. It might have made her life more difficult."

"You think so?"

"I do."

"When I heard she'd fallen to her death, I knew he was responsible. Oh, I doubt the big man, Enzo Massito, dirtied his hands, but someone pushed her out of that window."

"Do you know who?"

"I suspect the man I'd been dating."

"Why?"

"I don't know. But in the last few days we were together, he didn't act like the same guy. Once I caught him frowning at me. I think he'd been sent to try and get information about my family. He asked questions, but I thought nothing of it since we'd been dating for several months."

"What did you tell him?

"That I was estranged from them, and I'd had no contact in seven years." She hesitated, and then asked, "If I tell you something, can you keep it a secret?"

"I'll try, but I don't know what it is, and if it's illegal, I'd have to report it to the police."

She sighed. "Thanks for your honesty. My sister and I both left home when we found out how our father made his money. He and Massito were rivals. My Dad wasn't in as deep as the Massito organization, but he played a dangerous game.

"I suspect my sister married Enzo Massito to protect our family. I'm not sure Enzo knew she was part of our family, but he might have. Enzo may have threatened our family to make her marry him. Our Mom and brothers are still at home or nearby."

"Are you the only two who left home?"

"Yes."

"I believe he knew exactly who she was connected with and wanted to enjoy her and get rid of her afterward, especially if your father was a competitor" Madison said. "He'd see it as revenge on another gang."

"You may be right."

"Did you recognize anyone in the group who kidnapped Kathleen Cafferty?"

"Only my old boyfriend. I didn't have much time to look at the other men."

"We'll put guards on your house, and you need to stay at home until all this is over."

She bit the edge of her lip. "I don't want to lose my job."

"You won't. I'll suggest to the head nurse that you need the time off until we have these guys locked up."

"Thank you."

"No, thank you. What you've told me will help us deal with this situation. Is there any other information you remember that may help us, even if it seems unimportant?"

"He mentioned a cabin once, near a creek. He said we'd go there sometime, but we didn't."

"Any idea where it might have been?"

Hesitantly, she said, "Yes. When our relationship

ended, I got suspicious. I did a foolish thing. I followed him to see if he'd found someone else. I stayed way back from his car. He turned onto one of the old highways." She handed Madison a slip of paper. "I drew the directions as best I remembered. I lost him at the x mark."

Madison hugged her. "Thank you. You may have saved a life. I'm definitely going to have a police officer take you home and put a guard at your house until this is over." Madison dialed Scott's number and gave him a quick explanation of what the nurse said.

"We'll meet you downstairs and outside the front doors," Scott promised.

Once the others arrived, the nurse was taken to her home with two police officers to guard her. Cory, Ranger and Kijika got into Ranger's truck and headed toward Massito's home.

* * *

"There are lots of small towns some distance from the city," Scott said to Madison as he got into the police vehicle. "It's hard to say where she might be. When I gave her the necklace, I was thinking more of her getting into trouble in San Diego County."

"Let me call Tex and see if he's gotten any noise from her tracker." Madison punched in Tex's number.

He answered on the first ring. "I was getting ready to call you. It may be nothing, but a few minutes ago, I got a faint signal. Just tracked it to an area northwest of this guy's house, probably about fifty miles or so. I'll send the map to show you where. Other than that one blink, there's been nothing. I can't even be sure it's from her."

"Thanks, Tex. This may be just what we need." Madison hung up. When the map got to his phone, he showed it to Scott.

"I'll call for backup just in case, and we'll head on out that way," Scott said.

Madison contacted the others, relayed Tex's information and told them to continue to search Massito's house and grounds.

"I'm coming, too," Cory spoke up.

Madison made a quick decision. "Time is of the essence. Be waiting right in front by the road." he said.

CHAPTER 7

Kat tried not to shiver. She didn't want Massito's men to think she was afraid. Keeping her head up, she frowned at them.

"The police, FBI and others will come after me. You need to let me go, or you'll find yourself in prison for a long time. Judges don't like criminals who threaten police officers."

A large hand slapped her in the face. "Shut up, or I'll put a gag in your mouth so tight you'll wish you'd been quiet."

The man in the front seat laughed. "They'll never know where to look. No one knows where to find our cabin."

"Shut up, Henry. You talk too much. She's not going to get a chance to tell anyone. Once we get to the farm, all they'll see are potatoes coming up in the field."

Kat thought she'd be sick, but fought her bile down. *I'll concentrate on a plan to get away from them.*

"Here's the turnoff," the man in the front seat said.

"Do we kill her now?" Her jailer in the back seat appeared to find excitement in that idea.

Leaning against the back seat, she worked at the rope around her hands. Relief washed through her as she freed one, then the other, but she kept the cord in place. She wanted them to think she was still tied up. She worked on stretching the ties around her feet.

The took a turn fast and she fell against the door. Her guard yanked her back into place. He moved closer. She wrinkled her nose at the smell of sweat and some sickly cologne he'd used to cover up his body odor.

He yanked her face around, kissed her, and slipped his hand under her blouse and bra to squeeze her breast, hard. He wasn't thinking of anything but her, which gave Kat an idea.

Before she could have doubts, she grabbed his gun and shot him in the chest, and the driver in the head. The car ran off the road, throwing them around until it hit a small tree. By this time, she'd shot at the last man several times, but because the car bounced so much, she missed. He'd shot her once in the arm.

When he tried to get out of the car, Kat held her gun to his head. "Drop it, or I'll blow your brains out."

The man looked from his gun to hers. She saw when he realized she'd get her shot off first.

"Here," he handed the gun to her. "Enzo's got good lawyers; he'll get me out."

"Don't count on it. Now sit tight. Someone will find us soon."

* * *

Madison's phone rang as they stopped to pick up Cory. "Tex, do you have any new information for me?"

Cory jumped in the car as Tex answered.

"Whatever she's wearing gave out two more faint pings, then it went dead again."

Scott hit the accelerator.

"Send me what you have. We hope we're going in the right direction." Madison looked at the area Tex had marked on the map. "It looks like we may be on the right road."

Scott drove faster. The roads narrowed, but he kept his foot on the pedal.

Madison had only ever experienced this type of fear when his Dad got seriously ill. "If you don't slow down, one of the county deputies will stop us and may not care what reason we have for speeding in his county," he warned Scott.

"Damn, I didn't notice we'd hit ninety." Scott let up on the gas. A short distance later, he slowed even more.

"A car went off the road here, once or twice." This time he drove much slower.

"Looks like a car went completely off the road here." Cory pointed at the broken wire fence. "There's the vehicle by the tree."

Scott parked his car, and they all drew their guns.

Moving carefully over the downed wire fence, they slid down the embankment and moved cautiously across the pasture toward the vehicle.

"I don't see anyone," Cory said.

"Anyone in that car is probably hurt," Scott said.

Madison's heart thumped so hard he couldn't speak.

* * *

Kat slid down in the seat. Her arm hurt, and she tried not to throw up. The man in the front seat wasn't in much better shape, but he watched every movement she made. It was a contest to see who would be the first to pass out.

"I ought to go ahead and kill you," Kat said. *But I'd never do that to an unarmed man. I just need to hang on. Scott and all the police force must be looking for me by now. But will they find me out here in time?* Then Kat heard a voice she'd thought she might not ever hear again, she let out a sigh of relief.

"If anyone's in the car, raise your hands," Scott

yelled.

"It's me, Scott," she called out. "And I have the only gun."

Just then, the man who'd been staring at Kat for what seemed hours threw himself toward her. His hands clamped over the gun and he struggled to twist it out of her hand.

Scott and Madison ran to the side of the car and threw the front passenger door open. Madison grabbed the man from behind and wrenched the gun-free. Then he put the gun against the man's temple and growled, "Please move and try to take the gun back. I'd love to put a bullet in your head."

The guy sat back and raised his hands.

"Turn and put your hands behind your back," Madison said as Scott threw him a pair of handcuffs before lifting his sister out of the car and carrying her toward the road and his unmarked car.

When the guy was cuffed, Madison had him get out of the car and walk in front of him. By the time they reached the road, Scott had called for an ambulance, the local police, and for the dead men to be picked up and taken to the nearest morgue. Sirens sounded in the distance.

"They'll be here in a minute," Scott said. He glanced in the back seat of his car, where his sister lay with her head in Cody's lap.

The ambulance arrived first. The EMTs helped Kat onto a stretcher, loaded her in their vehicle and started towards the closest hospital, twenty miles away. When the police arrived, they took charge of the cuffed man and put him in a squad car. The sheriff sauntered over to Scott, Cory and Madison.

"Guess this is the most excitement we've had in the last twenty years. Old John killed his ornery wife back then. Can't say I blame him. Anyway, that was an open and shut case. He told us he was guilty and shot himself before we could have a trial."

Madison explained they'd been after the men who'd kidnapped Kat, a police detective and Scott and Cory's sister.

"Well, you did a good job," the sheriff said.

"We'll send you the proper paperwork and have one of our men pick the suspect up later tonight," Scott explained.

"I'd appreciate that. I'd have to look for extra deputies I don't have, to guard him until he gets released to you, so the quicker, the better."

They shook hands, and then Scott, Madison and Cory got in the unmarked car, checked their map and headed to the hospital where Kat had been transferred.

"Let's not tell Mom what's happened until we see Kat," Scott said. "If Kat's able, we'll drive her back to a hospital at home."

"Sounds like a good idea to me," Cory agreed.

"I'll stay with her until she gets transferred to San Diego and is safe," Madison added.

"Thanks. I have to get back and explain to my supervisor what we've been doing all day," Scott said and smiled. "He's going to rip my ass for not calling him before we went looking for Kat. I suspected he'd say we needed to call the local police. I had no intention of taking time for a lot of bureaucrat red tape."

"I would have gone on without you," Madison said.

"Me, too," Cory added.

"You didn't think I'd let two Navy SEALs have all the glory, did you?"

"Hell, yes," they both answered.

* * *

After her arm was bandaged, Kat lay on a bed in a small room. She had no idea where she was, and her arm hurt like blazes. A tall, grey-haired man knocked on the wall and walked into her cubicle.

"Miss Cafferty, I'm Dr. Raineau, an orthopedic surgeon. I've been asked to look at your arm. Do you mind?"

"No, go right ahead. It's hurting more than at first."

He gently took off the bandage. "Hmmm. How long since you were shot?"

"Honestly, I've lost count of the time. It seemed forever before I was rescued, but I don't think it was more than some hours, four, six, I don't know."

"We need to get the bullet out, and I'll start you on some antibiotics."

"When can I go home?"

He smiled. "All of my patients have the same question, and I always have the same answer — I don't know. I understand they'll want to transfer you to San Diego County as soon as possible, but I imagine you won't go from one hospital to another at least for a few days."

"Why?"

"You need antibiotics intravenously for a short time, to be on the safe side."

When Kat frowned, the physician smiled. "You remind me of my daughter when she fell and hurt her leg. No patience, she wanted to be well immediately."

"Did she become a doctor?"

"No, she had no desire to see all that blood and stuff, as she put it. She's done quite well in the business world."

"Good for her on doing her own thing."

"I need to see my other patients. You'll continue to be NPO, nothing by mouth, and I will see you in surgery in about two hours."

Scott called her from his phone. "I just got reamed

out by our boss, and you'll get it when you get back. It seems we ought to have taken time, and had more help investigating the situation."

"I might have been dead by then."

"Our boss seems to believe nothing can stop you, not bad guys, and certainly not the rules. You're in for it when you get back."

"He's pissed because he didn't get into the action and can't take any of the glory."

"I know, and you know, but he'd never admit it."

Kat explained she had to have the surgery and be transferred near home after she had intravenous antibiotics. "He thinks I might have an infection and wants to watch me for a few days. The way it hurts, he may be right."

"Mom will be glad to have you back in town. She'll want you to be on the mend before you go to her house."

"I'd like to go home and have no one bother over me."

"Yeah, lots of luck having that happen. I'm hanging up. We're getting close."

* * *

Kat had just put down the phone and closed her eyes. It seemed only a minute when she heard a knock on her door. Her eyes opened wide when Cory and Madison poked their heads inside.

"Can we join you?" Cory asked.

"Yes. How did you get here so fast?"

"We had to go back with Scott and get Madison's car. Then we drove faster than allowed to get back here and find you." Cory grinned and kissed his sister's forehead. "You always got in trouble for falling out of a tree or something when we were growing up, and you haven't changed a bit."

"I never will, bro."

She looked at Madison and tilted her head. "How did you get mixed up in all of this?"

"It's a long story I'll tell you some other time, but I wouldn't have missed it."

"If I'd had my gun in the drawer at the hospital, this would never have happened. Because of rules, the hospital staff took it away. I'll hide it better next time.

"I have to have surgery, and then hopefully be transferred to a hospital near home. The surgeon thinks I might need antibiotics. We'll see. Once he removes the bullet, I should be fine."

"Right," both men said at once and laughed.

"Go away. I want people to agree with me. I've been hurt, and the least you can do is sympathize with my condition."

For a minute, no one said anything, and then Cory and Madison laughed again. She shook her head and closed her eyes. "I get no respect."

"Look, I have to get back to base. I've contacted our Captain, and your brother will stay to protect you overnight. If I don't get called away, I'll be back in the morning."

"You might go on another mission so soon?" she asked, feeling disappointed.

"We never know. You're in good hands, and I'll probably be free to take over for the morning."

"You don't have to bother," she said and put her nose in the air.

He leaned down close and whispered, "It's not a bother." He kissed her quickly, waved at a smiling Cory, and hurried out of the room.

* * *

"I think you like him," Cory said. "If anyone else kissed you so soon, you'd hit them."

"You're right. I don't understand why I'm not pushing Madison away."

"Maybe he already means more to you than any of the others."

"Perhaps, but it'll never last. Madison will be like the rest and do something that annoys me. Or we won't be compatible in some way, and I'll tell him to get lost."

"From what I saw and heard, he's well respected by his team. They tease him, and their nickname for him is the Professor. Not sure why. He just laughs and shrugs it off."

"Can you tell me about what happened on your first mission?"

"Nope. But they said I did well."

"Do you really like it?"

"Absolutely."

"Aren't you scared? I mean, your job is more dangerous than most."

"Are you scared of being a detective?" He nodded at

her lying in bed. "It's dangerous. You're in the hospital waiting for surgery."

"All right, you got me. I think we Caffertys like a mix of action and danger. It's in our blood."

"Except for Lloyd. It's just as well he's doing his residency in surgery so he can sew the rest of us up when we're injured."

"Good point. Sis is a teacher. That's two children, out of six, Mom doesn't have to worry about in their career."

The door opened. A nurse wearing green scrubs and an orderly pushed a gurney into the room.

"We're going to take your sister to surgery," the nurse said. "You can follow us and sit in the waiting room."

"All right. Will the surgeon come out and speak to me afterward?"

"Do you agree?" she asked Kat.

"Oh, yes. If my brother doesn't call my mother, she'll be on the road headed this way."

"I'm already here."

Kat grinned and nodded at the door. "Meet my mother and father, Mrs. and Mr. Cafferty."

"We'll follow you up and sit with Cory."

The surgical nurse grinned. "Yes, Ma'am."

* * *

When Madison got home, he called his parents' number. His Dad answered.

"You sound good, Dad. How's it going?"

"I feel better than I have in years. How about you?"

"I've meant to call more since I got back from my mission, but I got involved with a case here in San Diego. The detective I told Mom about, the one who rescued me from being shot, was kidnapped from the hospital. I helped her brothers, one who's a SEAL and the other a detective, find her. It's a long story I'll explain more when you come for Christmas. You are going to be here, I hope."

"Yes, we're looking forward to the trip. We'll fly in a few days before the holiday and stay for a few days after. I have an appointment for a checkup on my heart on the twenty-ninth. We need to be back by then."

"Are you having any problems?"

"No, they just want to keep a close eye on me."

"I'll have your room ready for you, and plan something fun to do while you're here."

"We keep telling you, you don't have to entertain us."

"I know, but I like to see the smiles on Mom's face when we visit new places."

Madison hesitated. "Ah, and I'd like you to meet the detective who stopped me from being shot."

"Good, we'll thank her."

"Okay, Dad. See you soon." He put down the phone and went into the kitchen, where he turned on his coffee pot. Bright sunlight shone through the window. He walked over and looked out into his yard as the smell of coffee brewing filled the room.

I need to distance myself from Kat. I've only made quick decisions a few times, and each time was a mistake. Once was when I married my first wife. I can't get too attached to

Kat. I don't know her well enough, and she has a dangerous job.

He turned and poured himself a cup of coffee, breathed in the smell, and took a sip. In the living room, he kicked off his shoes, sprawled out on the sofa and stared up at a picture of his parents. He wanted a marriage like theirs. It had lasted forty years. He'd heard all about how they met in high school and dated no one else.

He groaned and put his head in his hands. *But how can I change my feelings for Kat? They're getting stronger every day.*

* * *

"I needn't have worried about being busy over Christmas," Madison said to his Captain. "With so many gone for the holidays, there's been plenty to do cleaning up around here."

"I hope you don't mind getting the clean-up jobs," Captain Buchanan said.

"No way. They filled in for me so I could be with Mom and Dad."

"Are your parents coming for Christmas?"

"Yes. Dad's doing well, and they want to see me."

"You're all welcome to join us Christmas Day, if you can handle three children running around excited."

"Sounds great, but I got a call from Mrs. Cafferty yesterday. She insisted my parents and I join their family for Christmas. I tried to get out of it, but she wouldn't let me."

"They sound like a great group. You may enjoy yourself more than you expect."

"They have six grown children, and I believe she said six grandchildren. My parents and I have few relatives, and usually we have a quiet Christmas. I couldn't say no."

"Let me know how it goes. I'd love to be a fly on the wall," Buchanan said and laughed.

At home, Madison thought about the conversation with his Captain and wondered if his folks would enjoy such a large family gathering.

He'd kept in touch to see how Kat was doing, but gave excuses for why he didn't go by the hospital to see her when she was transferred back to San Diego after her surgery. *Having so many guys on vacation for the holidays gave me the perfect excuse to stay away. Hopefully, by the time I see her again, my feelings will have calmed down. Then I can treat her like she's just a friend and not someone I want to kiss every time she's around.*

His cell rang. "Scott, what's up?"

"Can you come to the police station one day this week or next? I need your account of what we found and did when we rescued Kat. It's just a formality, but if the guy goes to trial, you may have to be a witness."

"I'll be glad to help, but I may not be in town when he goes on trial. I'm sure you have an idea from your brother how we may have to leave at a minute's notice."

"We'll just have to use your sworn statement in that case. Be sure and include all you can remember."

"Will do. I go in late tomorrow, so I'll come in early in the morning. Is that all right?"

"Sure. I'll let the proper people know." He sounded uncomfortable as he said, "Ah, Kat said you haven't been around lately. She got discharged today and is wanting to come back to work, at least on desk duty. I love her, but she's so stubborn."

"I've noticed that. I'm sure you can handle your sister better than anyone."

"I don't know. I thought you might go by and say hello and encourage Kat to rest and relax."

"I'm pretty busy. I don't think Kat would listen to me anyway. Tell your Mom. She'll tie her to the bed."

Scott laughed. "You're most likely right. I'll call Mom. I did think you two were getting close, but you stopped coming around, so..."

"Most of my team's on vacation. Since I had so much time off when my Dad had his operation, I'm filling in for them."

"I see. I'll explain your disappearance to Kat. Bye." He hung up abruptly.

Damn, they all noticed our attraction to each other. I guess I'd better visit Kat and make amends, or Christmas may be awkward.

He half-hoped her mother's car would be parked outside her condo, but no such luck. Otherwise, he'd have driven on by. After parking, Madison rode up the elevator to the fourth floor and knocked on her door.

"If you don't have a key, you're not welcome," Kat yelled out.

"Okay, see you later," Madison shouted back.

"Wait. It'll take me time to get to the door."

"Have you got a chain lock?"

"No, why?

"Stay there." Madison pulled out a little kit most of the SEALs often carried with them. Within two minutes, he had the door open. He walked through the small foyer to the living room.

"What the hell? How did you do that?"

"Most clever crooks could get in. You need a much better lock on your front door. I'll pick one up later and come back tomorrow to put it on."

"I was told that was the best they had, and I really didn't pay much attention. I know, I'm a cop and should have noticed. But I don't spend much time at home."

"Maybe it was a good lock years ago, but not now. Who told you?"

"The condo supervisor."

"I'll give you the bill to show her. Tell her all the condos will need the type I'm bringing you tomorrow."

"All right. Sit down. It's been a long time since your last visit. I thought you were mad at me."

"I was for a while. You're too headstrong and think you can handle everything. You have a team of police officers to help. Why go out on your own?"

"This time, they came for me, remember? I was minding my own business in my hospital bed. It was planned, and they got away with no problem."

"I had forgotten the full circumstances," Madison lied. *I hadn't, but I want her to think what I said was true, instead of her knowing she'd been constantly on my mind.* "If I weren't so sleepy that day, I'd have been with you."

"You, Scott and Cory found me, that's what is important."

"How's the arm?"

"There's still some pain. I can handle it, but lying around my house is driving me crazy. I need to work, even if it's only in a room at headquarters."

"What are your hobbies? Now's a good time to enjoy them."

"I like archery, can't do that. Boating is also out. I do love reading and taking interesting classes."

"Do you have any books to read?"

"No, I've finished all the ones I have at home."

"My mother says I have a huge library. It's not that big, but I have quite a few books. I'll bring some over tomorrow when I bring the lock, and I've been taking a bridge class. How about being my partner, and we can learn together."

"Who's teaching it?"

"My Captain's wife. We'll go to his house tomorrow night, have dinner and play bridge. They have children, but they'll go to bed before we start the bridge classes."

"Sounds like fun." She studied him and tipped her head to the side.

"What?"

"Did Scott put you up to this?"

"Only to a visit, not the suggestions I made."

"Okay. I think."

"I have to go and complete a report about our rescue, and then report to base. I'll be here tomorrow afternoon, fix your lock, and we'll go learn how to play bridge."

"I can hardly wait."

Madison raised one eyebrow. "Are you being snarky?"

Kat smiled. "No, you are saving my sanity."

He wanted to lean down and kiss her, but he backed away and headed for the door. "See you soon." Waving, he snapped the lock in and closed the door, and then took the stairs down two at a time.

You'd think I was running from a bad guy, but I'm rushing away from temptation. This will be harder than I thought. He opened his car door, got in, and pulled out of the parking area bound for the police station. *I can't get my head and heart to work together.*

CHAPTER 8

When Madison arrived at Kat's apartment the next day, she was up and dressed. "I had to see my doctor today, so I left my good clothes on. It's an effort to put my blouses on with this arm."

"You look good." Madison held up her new door lock. "It won't take me long to install this one. I brought an extra one for you to show to the head of the condos."

"Thanks." Kat sat on the sofa and watched him work. "Did your Dad teach you how to do things around the house?"

Madison nodded. "He did. He said a son or daughter needed to know some basic work that might need to be done to the house and car or truck."

"My Dad felt the same way. My sister, Deirdre, and I were both included in their lessons needed for life, as Mom and Dad called them. That meant the boys had to learn to cook and clean, too."

"Smart parents. They sound like mine. I learned to cook and simple sewing, like putting buttons back on."

"We may have a larger family, but it sounds like our parents agreed on the way to raise children, whether it was one or six."

"There, the lock is on." He stood up and packed up the few tools he'd used. "I feel better knowing this one is much safer than the old one. Guess we'd better leave. Niall and Emma will be calling soon if we don't."

When Madison opened the door of his car for Kat, she asked, "You call your Captain by his first name and visit him and his wife. It seems unprofessional in away. I sure don't want to have dinner and play bridge with my Unit Supervisor and his wife."

"Why not?"

"Most detectives just don't mix with the boss much, and if we do, it's at our favorite bar to have a drink."

Madison nodded and closed her door. There wasn't much conversation on the way to the Captain's house.

"We're almost there," Madison said. "Is your arm doing okay?"

"Yes, I'm fine. I can almost hear the wheels in your head, turning over regarding our previous conversation."

"I am. Our groups are different. SEALs respect and certainly obey orders from our Captain, but when we're home, we're much more relaxed and often socialize with each other. There have been many times when our Captain and his wife joined us at Aces Bar and Grill."

"Is he nice?"

"Except when you do something wrong or stupid. Then you never do it again."

"So, all friendliness is gone?"

"Oh, yes. And you never want to go see the Commander. That's really bad."

She laughed. "I'd bet you've never had to go."

"Why?"

"There's a seriousness about you, and I believe you're knowledgeable in many subjects. It just wouldn't go with what I've seen of your personality."

"Ah, so you've been analyzing me."

"I'm sorry. My family gets mad when they catch me doing it. I studied psychology in college."

"I can't be mad. I've been doing the same thing about you."

"Really? And what are your conclusions about me?"

Madison pulled into a driveway and parked. "No time, we're here." He went around to her door and opened it.

She narrowed her eyes up at him. "Don't think you'll get away without answering my question. It's a long drive home."

"What if I know a shortcut?"

"I won't let you out of the car until I have an answer."

He looked her up and down, and her body heat rose. *There's probably smoke coming out of my ears.* Kat grinned. "I can be quite a devil."

"I'm counting on it." Now his eyes sparkled with mischief.

"Let's go to the door before they come outside looking for us."

He brushed her hair back from her face. "You're beautiful, even when you're annoyed."

Just in time, the door opened. "Are you two planning on staying outside all evening? We can bring the food out here," Emma teased.

Niall stepped up behind her. "Don't tease, honey. They're just getting to know each other."

"True," Emma said. "Oh, look. They're both blushing."

"Come on in, before my wife has both your faces red. She loves to tease."

They stepped into the house, and Madison introduced Kat. "Her real name is Kathleen."

Kat looked at him. "How do you know that?"

"I heard your Mom call you Kathleen."

"She's the only one, well, and Dad, who don't call me Kat."

"Another new fact I learned about you."

To Emma, she said, "Thank you for letting me join the group. I don't know how to play bridge."

"No problem. I can help you, and Niall will help Madison. But first, dinner."

After dinner, they played bridge and laughed at the newbies, but it was all fun. Madison watched Kat.

It's the first time I've seen her this relaxed, and she's a quick learner. I've had to work on learning the game to keep up with her. I like intelligent women, and I'm afraid I'm beginning to love her.

Emma stood. "This has been a delightful evening. I'll get our coffee, and we can relax before you two call it a night. These guys have to go to work tomorrow."

"True," Niall said and kissed her cheek as he stood, too. "I'll help you with the coffee."

Emma raised her eyebrows. "I don't need help."

"I know. I like to get in the way."

Emma blushed and went to the kitchen with Niall right behind her.

"Be back soon," Niall called over his shoulder.

Kat looked at Madison. "Are they newlyweds?"

"No, they just adore each other. But they're discreet when out with strangers. They must like you to trust you not to tell anyone else about their behavior."

"I think it's great. Mom and Dad act silly and loving all the time."

"Mine, too. Maybe that's what makes a strong marriage," Madison said. He leaned close and nuzzled her neck.

She jumped. "What are you doing?"

"Nuzzling your neck. It's rather delectable."

"If we weren't here, I'd punch you."

"I don't think so. I see the pulse beating rapidly in your neck." He leaned forward and kissed the area.

Kat jolted out of her chair and walked across the room.

"Was I wrong?"

"About what?"

"I thought you'd enjoy what I did."

"Of course not. We're only acquaintances."

Madison strolled in her direction. He stopped when their bodies almost touched. She gulped, and he smiled.

"I do believe I've rattled my Amazon detective."

"No, you haven't. We don't know each other very well, and you are invading my space."

"I'd have sworn you were ready for me to move

closer. Sorry," Madison turned and walked to the chair across from her. He liked teasing her and seeing her flustered. It softened her usual proper formal appearance.

"I hope we didn't take too long making the coffee," Emma said, her cheeks rosy with a blush.

"Not at all. We decided to move into the living room and make ourselves comfortable." Madison sat on the chair across from Kat and caught the flash of irritation in her eyes. He smiled and winked. *Ah, she's sizzling angry. I'd like to make love to her, right now, but I'm sure Niall and Emma might disapprove.*

"Would you prefer coffee or wine, Kat?" Niall asked. "We thought coffee might keep you awake if you have to get up early."

"I'll be fine without either. I'm still on some medication.

"Let me get you some water or lemonade, which would you like?" Emma asked.

"Lemonade sounds great." Kat smiled at Niall and said, "Your wife is sweet."

Niall grinned. "It's part of the reason I married her."

Emma returned with the lemonade and sat beside Niall with her hand on his knee. "When do you think you'll be able to return to work?" she asked.

"I'm supposed to be on leave until my shoulder heals, but I plan on going to the office and talking with my partner about our last case."

"Will you Mom drive you to work?" Madison asked.

"I can take the bus. It stops right across the street from my condo."

Madison didn't comment.

As soon as they finished their beverages, Kat suggested they head home. When she stood, Emma hugged her.

"It's more fun with all four of us. You must come with Madison the next time we play "bridge."

"I enjoyed the evening, but my shifts change often. If I'm not on a call for work, I'd love to enjoy getting more lessons and seeing you and your husband."

"Well, I hope we get to see more of you," Emma said. "All of you have such demanding jobs, but you are protecting the world and San Diego," she said and hugged Kat again.

* * *

Madison took Kat's keys and unlocked the door of her condo. He waited to be invited inside. *Maybe she is angry with me.*

"Come on in. You look sad standing there waiting for an invite."

"Not sad. Hopeful."

As the entered the living room, Kat said, "I don't know what you are, hop—"

Madison's lips on hers stopped the word as he pulled her into his arms. She tasted sweet and sexy. He pulled her closer against his body until they were locked in a tight embrace. One hand cupped her breast, and his finger moved across her nipple. Her body shook, and she moaned softly.

Then she pushed him away and rushed into the kitchen.

"How about coffee?" When she spoke, her voice trembled.

Madison stood in the doorway. "What happened? Did I offend you in some way?"

When she looked at him, her face was flushed and her eyes clouded with pain. He felt like an ass.

"I'm sorry if I hurt your arm. I must admit I forgot all about it."

"It's fine."

"Then what? I thought you were enjoying our touching and kissing as much as I was."

She gulped. "I did, but it's best for two people who are devoted to their jobs, as we are, not to get so involved."

"Who told you that was a good idea?"

"My ex-husband."

"Is he a police officer? Does he work in your department?"

"Not now. After our divorce, he transferred to the Sheriff's Department."

"Was that your suggestion or his idea?"

"Why all these questions?"

"I'm attracted to you, and your behavior confuses me. Sometimes you draw away, and at other times you seem more open to us having a relationship."

Kat turned to the coffee maker and set it up to perk. Then she spent more time than was strictly necessary washing her hands. She didn't look at Madison.

If I do, I'll want to fall into his arms, and I don't plan to place my heart in another man's hands.

Her ex-husband's words when he walked out the door two years ago still rang in her ears.

"You're unnatural, more like a man. Your job, and your competition with your brothers and, let's not forget, the lame way you make love."

When he laughed, her heart broke and hardened as he slammed the door behind him.

I promised myself I'd never let another man get close, but this man is difficult to forget and keep away.

"You must be having deep, serious thoughts. Want to share?"

"No, I'm fine. But my career comes first, so I prefer not to date a man I might come to like too much."

"Ah, so you *do* like me. I've had the same thoughts about relationships, but since meeting you, I'm changing my mind. I want to learn more about you." He moved closer and settled his hands at her waist. "And I want to make love to you."

"I'm not good at it."

"Good at what?"

"Making love."

He laughed, and she flinched. "I'm sorry. But whoever gave you that idea means the problem was his. I can taste your sexuality in your kiss, and the thought of making love to you makes me ache with desire."

"You'd laugh at me and walk out the door."

"What? Did your ex-husband make you feel that way?"

She blinked quickly and lowered her head, hoping he wouldn't notice her tears.

He did. Madison tipped her face up and kissed the tears away. "Tell me his name. I'd like to give him a good beating."

She smiled at the fierceness in his tone. "You mustn't ever do such a thing. It'd get you both in trouble."

"For me, it'd be worth it."

"I think I'd like to see it, but no."

"All right, but you have to give me a chance to show you what a sexy woman you are."

"Maybe when we know each other better."

"The more you put it off, the more difficult it will be for you to relax with any man. We'll go slow. If you tell me to stop, I promise I will."

His eyes showed so much of who he was, and Kat knew if ever she trusted a man again, he was the one she'd believe told the truth. She put out her hand, and he took it.

"Show me the way," he said.

She grinned. "I'm certain in this condo, a SEAL will have no trouble leading me to my room."

Madison swept her into his arms and walked down the hall. He stood in the doorway of her bedroom.

"Are you waiting for my permission to go inside?" she asked.

"Partly. I'm also stunned at your feminine room. I never expected pink and ruffles and stuffed animals."

"If I'd known you were going to talk me into this, I'd have hidden them."

"I love it. You hide your femininity behind the walls of your private escape."

She raised her eyes to his face. "You don't think it's childish or foolish?"

"No. It shows a side I suspect you are afraid to show others. Do *you* think it shows weakness?"

A memory she thought she'd forgotten came into her mind as though it was yesterday. Scott had teased her when she asked to join her Dad and brothers in boy games, as Scott called them, or climbing trees with them.

"Girls don't get to climb trees and play football or any boy games. You need to go with Mom and Deirdre, so they can help you learn feminine things," her oldest brother said with authority, and all the boys laughed.

"You just went pale. Did I say something wrong?"

"No, I just had a memory suddenly go through my mind."

"Was it embarrassing?"

"Sort of, but I'm glad you like my room."

"I do. It suits the side of you that I'm certain you show to only a few people."

"Yes, you're right."

She took his hand and smiled. "If you come into my bedroom, I may catch you in my web."

"I have no fear of being caught in your web. I think I'll like it. Later, I'll tell you who wrote the poem and how the sentence really goes."

"All right, Professor."

Madison laughed and lifted her into his arms. "Whatever you want, my dear."

Kat laughed, and looking into his face, her heart raced. *I have more to fear than I thought. He's the first man to make me laugh so freely, and my body respond to him so quickly.*

"No negative thoughts. Throw them all away and start new with me."

"It might be dangerous for both of us."

He dropped Kat on the bed and lay beside her fully clothed. Then he nuzzled her neck and kissed the place where her heart raced. She scrunched her neck up.

"I'm ticklish there."

"Oh, you should never have told me that," he teased. His expression grew more serious as he slowly unbuttoned her blouse and kissed each spot as it was laid bare.

"Your skin is as soft as the first snow that falls, but warm as velvet." When he uncovered her breasts, he cupped them in his hands.

"They aren't big," she whispered.

"I suppose your asshole of an ex-husband said that to you."

"Right." She swallowed the nervous laugh that tried to come out.

"He was stupid, and he lost you. I'm smart."

This did make her laugh, and he grinned. Madison leaned up to kiss her lips again. "Lovemaking should be full of laughter and wonder. I like the sound when you laugh."

Suddenly, she pushed him over to his back. "It's about time your clothes came off.

"What do you say we stand up and undress. I'm ready to kiss you all over."

His words made her tremble with desire. "I'm ready." She jumped up and yelled, "The last one in bed is a slowpoke."

She blinked at how fast he got naked.

Lying in bed, smiling, he opened his arms. "Come on, I can't wait to hold your naked body against mine."

"I'm not slow." She swung one of her legs across his body and leaned down to bite the edge of his ear. Then her kisses rained on his body as she moved downward.

He quickly rolled her over and spread her legs. "I'm going to burst if I wait any longer." He reached over to get the condom he'd placed on the bedside table and rolled it on. Then he leaned down, kissed her lips, and his hard cock slid slowly into her tightness.

When he settled deep inside her, he whispered in her ear, "Don't listen to those negative thoughts in your head. You are a hot mama."

She looked into his eyes, and something deep inside her shifted. It was as though a tightness she thought would never go away loosened, freeing warm, sexy feelings. Hot blood raced in her veins. For a second, fear almost stopped the response.

As though he knew, Madison whispered, "Let go. I won't let you be hurt. You are an insanely sexy woman." When he raised his head, his smile warmed her throughout.

His cock stroked inside her, fast and hard. "Come with me, sexy lady."

When feelings held so tightly exploded inside her,

she raised her hips and moved with him until she reached a pinnacle she'd never experienced. Afterward, they lay side by side, sweaty and trembling.

"Damn, woman. You might have killed me, but I'd die happy."

"No way you'd go that easy, my fantastic SEAL."

"Let's take a shower, and after we sleep a bit, we'll see if we can duplicate what we just did."

"I can. The question is, can you?" She laughed at his surprised expression and ran to the shower.

CHAPTER 9

They met every night she wasn't working and talked and made love. It was as though a barrier broke inside her.

"I can't understand what happened to me. Even my Mom says I seem different, more relaxed, and happy."

"What did you tell her?" Madison asked.

Kat sat up on her knees on the couch and leaned against him. "I told her I was madly in love, and we enjoyed wild sex every night." She fell over laughing at his expression. Madison had to grab her to keep her from falling on the floor.

"You didn't," he said, his face red.

"No, but I wanted to."

"I fear she might have told my mother, thinking it was funny."

"How would your Mom take it?" Kat sat back on her heels.

"I don't know. We had a lot of laughter in our home, but nothing risqué."

"Ah, so you're a prude at heart."

He started tickling her. "Am I a prude?"

"Not with me, thank goodness. We may need to slow things down a bit, though."

"Why?" he asked and wrinkled his forehead.

"People are asking why I'm smiling so much more and apparently not being such a hard-ass."

"You'd give us up so you can be seen as a 'hard ass'?"

She laughed and leaned against him again. "You are so funny. Part of you wants to let go more, and the other part is the Professor or Prof that the guys call you, examining everything."

"If I let go any more, we might die in each other's arms." He kissed her on the nose.

"True."

"I'm surprised that you like to read and learn new things as much as I do, and you like archery. I think we may be made for each other." When he made the last statement, he watched her face.

She sobered. "Ah, maybe we are moving a bit fast."

"So you are just taking advantage of me?"

"Are you serious?" Then she shook her head and said, "No, we're taking advantage of each other. I don't want to be too serious about anyone. This is fun, but … let's keep it light."

"You're right, and I need to sleep in my own bed for a change. My folks are arriving in two days. So I'll stay home and make certain the house is good and clean." He shifted her away from him. "I'll see you at the Christmas party."

"That's three days away," she said and looked puzzled.

"Yes, it is." He quickly dressed, opened her door, and waved goodbye.

In his car, Madison sat for a moment and banged his fist on the steering wheel. Then he started the car and raced down the street.

Damn, I knew better than to rush her, but I thought she felt the same as I did. She's right. It's too soon for either of us to be getting serious. He told himself a breather would do them both good. *Liar.*

* * *

Kat arrived at the station around ten o'clock. She thought her supervisor would be away from his office, as he usually was at this time of day. *I was wrong.*

He stood in her doorway and scowled. "What the hell are you doing here? You're supposed to be taking care of your shoulder and arm."

"I'm much better, and I can't stand staying in my condo any longer. Can't I help answering phones and dealing with paperwork?"

"I don't trust you. A call comes in, and you'll believe you can handle it. Anyway, I've put another detective working with Marcos."

"Not permanently."

"Perhaps. I'll see how Marcos likes his new partner. I am concerned that you aren't the best person to be a detective. You're too volatile, like to make your own decisions, and give me heartburn." His frown deepened.

"I get the job done." She swallowed hard. *I must show no weakness to this man.*

"Yes, in your own way. But it often involves putting yourself and others in danger."

Kat's back stiffened. Her heart raced, and her head spun. She'd never expected to be set back in her career. Anger churned inside her, but she knew any evidence of losing her cool would be held against her.

"Then put me on probation. Let me show you I can do better."

His dark eyes studied her. "I doubt any of you Caffertys can follow orders. Your brother does better than you, but he walks a fine line."

"Do you have something against the Caffertys?"

"Hell, no. Your Dad was a great chief, but you aren't like him. You're an impetuous person, certain your way is the best, and you don't obey orders well."

Anger rolled through her and her body trembled. She tried to bite her lip and keep her mouth shut. Her mother once told her she did a poor job of it. Looking at her boss, she said, "I will quit before I'm demoted."

"Then put in your papers to leave."

Stunned, she looked at him and took a deep breath. "Just like that?"

"Yes. Quit trying to be like your brother. You're a woman, behave like one, and go gracefully."

Her hand was in the air before she knew it. The slap left a red hand mark on her boss's cheek.

He blinked and shouted. "Get out of here now, and go to the Personnel Office. I'll call them and let the manager know you are terminated." He turned and walked back into his office. When he slammed the door, the glass rattled.

Kat turned to look around the room. There was silence, and everyone quickly turned their heads and tried to pretend they were working.

Holding her head high, Kat strode out of the room, her posture stiff. *It's the longest walk of my life.* Tears blurred her eyesight. When she tried to swallow, she couldn't. Once outside the room, she got on an empty elevator going down. *I can hold on until I get to my car,* she kept repeating to herself. *I knew he never liked me, but I got my work done and swiftly. He stunned me when he spoke so negatively about my work. Scott has done the same, but he's a man.*

She crumpled to the floor just as the elevator door opened. Scott stood waiting. Without a word, he scooped her up and carried her to his car.

"I have my car here," she protested.

"You are in no shape to drive. I'll take you to see Mom."

She reached down to open the door. He helped her into the car and put on her seatbelt. Then he went around to the driver's side. "Want to tell me what happened?"

"You must know. You're here."

"One of your friends in the office called me. I knew our boss didn't like you for some reason, but I never expected him to fire you."

"I guess it was partially my fault and my mouth."

Scott shook his head. "I expect it was, but you do

good work, a bit unorthodox at times, but you don't break the rules."

A brief grin came across her face. "I just bend them as far as I can."

"Some supervisors would appreciate that type of detective, but our supervisor goes by the book. He never did so well as a detective, and I suspect since he's the cousin of our Commander, he got help getting the promotion."

"I can tell my side to personnel. Oh, I was supposed to go there before I left." She reached for the door handle.

"Don't. Later will be better. You'll be more in control of yourself."

She leaned back in the seat. "I guess you're right. Take me to see Mom. I'm sure you called her."

"Yes, but I didn't say much. I left that for you."

"Thanks, Scott."

He started the car and waited to pull out onto the street. Scott glanced at her. "Why do you feel you have to challenge every man? Are you sorry you were born a woman?" He pulled out into the side lane and waited for her reply.

Finally, she said, "I don't know."

"Maybe you'd do better if you thought about that question and came up with an answer."

"Perhaps."

Kat closed her eyes. She didn't want to talk anymore and her head had started to ache.

When the car stopped, she opened her eyes.

"You weren't asleep?"

"No, I was thinking about what you said. Thanks for the advice, big brother."

He smiled. "If I didn't have a family, I'd quit my job in protest over how you were treated."

She leaned forward and kissed his cheek. "I know, and I love you for it. Stay in the car. I'll get out and go talk with Mom." She reached over and hugged him, then got out of the car and waved as he drove off.

Kat walked into the kitchen, where her mother spent a lot of time. She loved to cook and had taught both daughters how to cook and bake, despite Kat trying her best to get out of the lessons.

When her Mom turned and simply opened her arms, Kat ran to her and cried. The warmth of her mother's hug reminded Kat of all the times Mom had kissed away the small hurts from cuts and bruises. But this time was different. Kat had lost her way.

"I've made tea, and your favorite peanut butter cookies are in the oven. Go wash your face and relax in the family room. I'll bring the tea and cookies in shortly."

"How do you do it, Mom? You're always ready when one of us needs you."

Mom smiled. "Tea is quick to fix, and I already had mixed the cookies. Your favorite just happened to be the flavor for today. Now go wash your face and hands."

Kat looked in the bathroom mirror and was shocked at her appearance. Her hair stood out around her face.

My eyes are red, and I look like a different woman from the one who left for work this morning. She washed her face, found a comb in the purse she'd clung to all morning, then added more lipstick, which only made her skin seem paler.

Her mother had put the teapot, cups and cookies on her tea trolley and rolled it into the family room.

"I think the trolley must be one of your favorite gifts from Dad."

"Yes. He knew how I loved Regency romances, and I'd mentioned I wished I had a trolley to carry our snacks into the family room. I never expected to get one. He surprised me that Christmas. But let's talk about you."

"Must we? I've been fired, partially my mouth's fault." Kat tried to smile, but failed.

"Which doesn't surprise me. You got in more trouble in school because of your mouth than any of your brothers."

"My temper comes up, and I can't seem to stop my tongue from lashing out."

"You weren't that way when you were younger, but when you were around eleven, you started wanting to compete with your brothers. Deirdre never had that problem. Why do you suppose you do?"

"I wish I knew."

"Did something happen to you that made you want to be as strong as your brothers? I remember when you liked dolls and to spend time in the kitchen with your sister and me. Then you changed. You insisted on competing with the boys and threw all your, as you put it, girly things out, such as the dolls you'd loved."

"Nothing happened, Mom. It's just my disposition."

"I don't believe it. Whatever changed, you must have hidden it deep inside."

"Mom, you're silly. I love you. I'm fine. I like to do things for myself and be strong. There's nothing wrong with a woman wanting to compete with the men around her."

"No, there isn't, but you often take it further than you ought to, as I believe happened today."

"I did. Once I get furious, my mouth takes over."

"Think about when you started feeling threatened, and why that brings on the anger." Her mother brushed a hand across Kat's cheek. "I want you to be happy. I don't think you will be until you let yourself remember what happened to cause you to change so much."

Kat quickly drank her tea and ate two cookies. "I guess I'm not as recovered as I thought. My shoulder and arm are hurting, and a headache is coming on. I'd better call for a Uber to take me home."

"I can drive you."

"No, you'll want to start dinner soon."

"I'll drive her."

She blinked twice at the sound of Madison's voice, shocked to see him walk in. He smiled at her mother.

"Oh, I've so happy to see you again. You always seem to be around when Kathleen has a problem."

"How did you know I was here?" Kat asked. "Oh, I know. Scott called you."

"Yes, and Captain Buchanan said to take the rest of the day off and stay with you."

"Really, I'll punch my brother when I see him for disturbing so many people on my behalf."

Madison shrugged. "He's a good brother, and I didn't mind at all."

Kat kissed her Mom goodbye and groused under her breath as they walked to Madison's car. He opened the door, and she frowned. When he got into his seat, she said, "An Uber ride would have been fine. You didn't have to rearrange your whole day for me."

"No, but I wanted to be with you."

"Why? Because of the sex?"

His hand cupped her face and he made her look at him. "You insult yourself and me with that comment. I care about you, and I'd like to discover why you're so afraid to show your softer, feminine side."

"I don't have a softer side."

"Yes, you do." He let go of her face and started the car. "We'll talk more at your condo."

"My head hurts."

"I'll find something in your medicine cabinet to ease your pain."

"Men. You're all so bossy."

"And so are you."

There was silence between them for the rest of the drive.

When they reached her place, Kat went straight to her bathroom and took two pills. "I'm going to lie down and sleep. You can go or stay. I don't care."

Madison stood in front of her. "I'll be in the living room."

"You'll get bored."

"Don't worry about me. As a SEAL, I'm used to being quiet and waiting. Anyway, I saw some interesting books in your bookcase the other day. I like to read."

* * *

He shut the door and walked to the kitchen to make coffee. But as he sat later with the coffee and a book, his mind wandered to Kat. He had many questions about her.

He loved solving puzzles, and she was one. *I'm determined to discover the answers. Whatever it is concerns her determination to act more like a man and react that way to situations. I suspect the only problem her supervisor had with Kat was that he didn't know how to handle her.*

Madison forced himself to read the book he'd chosen. It was good, but he had difficulty concentrating with Kat in the other room.

He peeked in on her. She thrashed back and forth on the bed, mumbling incoherently. Madison quickly kicked off his shoes and slipped into bed beside her. He moved against her back and put his arm lightly around her.

"It's okay, Kat. I'm here. I won't let anyone hurt you."

She whispered something. He leaned close to hear her words, but couldn't make them out.

* * *

A too-frequent dream had Kat in its clutches.

"Thank goodness, I see my brothers. Get away from me."

"Ha, not before we have some fun." One boy squeezed her

breast. It hurt. He'd pushed her against his friend. They hadn't noticed Scott and Gavin running toward her. My brothers to my rescue. I'll be safe now.

Scott and Gavin yelled, "What the hell do you think you're doing to our sister?" They knocked down all three boys with their first punches. "Come on, Kat, we'll walk home with you from now on."

I need to make them promise not to tell Mom and Dad or my other brothers and sister. I don't want any more trouble.

She startled and only realized she was crying when Madison pulled her closer. "You're safe. Those boys will never hurt you again."

Kat's eyes popped open. "You invaded my space and listened to my words while I slept."

"You were mumbling and tossing and turning. I hoped to comfort you and, yes, even though you were not speaking distinctly, I think I understood some of what happened. I'm almost certain your brothers did as you asked and didn't tell your parents. That was a mistake."

She shrugged. "I knew some things on them that they'd rather Dad didn't know. I bribed them."

"And then you became determined to become so strong you could fight anyone and never let your guard down. What better way to get back at the boys who scared you than by becoming a police officer."

"You think you're so smart. Most of my family has been involved with the police force in one way or another until this generation. Scott and I were the only two to join the police force. Gavin is a fireman, and I think you know Lloyd is doing his residency to be an

Internist. He'll be the first doctor in the family, just like Cory is our first SEAL."

As they talked, she'd turned to lean against Madison's chest. Her fingers slid upward and brushed against his shiny black hair. Then her fingers moved to his cheekbone and, at last, she traced his lips.

"Your headache must be better. If it isn't, you'd better stop now."

"Or?"

He rolled her onto her back and held her hands above her head. "Or I will make love to you. Like this." His teeth bit lightly along her earlobe, and she shivered. Then he brushed his lips across her cheek. She'd closed her eyes and lay silently under him.

"So, *do* you have a headache?"

"It seems to have disappeared," she purred in his ear.

"Wonderful news." He quickly stood up, undressed and pulled a condom from his pocket. When he got back on the bed, he pulled her up enough to remove her thin nightgown. "You can tell me to stop at any time."

"Good to know. My ex-husband and I didn't have that agreement, and when I tried to use it, he ignored me. Our divorce was almost final, but he said I was unresponsive, and he'd try one more time to make me a woman."

"If I ever meet him, I promise he'll have those words rammed down his throat."

"Such a caveman. Stop talking and make love to me."

"Your wish is my command."

When he finally put the condom on and slid into her

heat, she was shaking, and he groaned. Their bodies seem to know what the other wanted without speaking.

Afterward, Madison held Kat close and kissed the top of her head. "You may try to hide your feminine side, but honey, you are all woman. Your ex-husband was crazy. I wish you'd accept your feminine side and find out what you really want to do with the rest of your life."

"I think that was what my mother was trying to suggest."

"How old were you when those boys attacked you?"

"Eleven. I'd been advanced in school, so I was a bit younger than my classmates. Luckily, Gavin and Scott happened to walk home that way. They didn't always. I'm certain my tormentors didn't expect to see them."

"You know those boys would have been punished if you'd only told your parents."

"Yes, but it was embarrassing enough that my brothers saw what was happening. I cried. I didn't want anyone else to know and have all that attention. That's mostly why they kept quiet." She took a deep breath. "Can't we talk about something else?"

"Yes. For now."

"You aren't going to let this go, are you?"

"We'll talk about it later."

She leaned up and kissed him. "I feel better with the sleep, even if it was restless. Now I have to think about another job."

"If you have savings and can take your time, do."

"I will. Right now, I'm too exhausted to think about anything but what I'll eat for dinner." She got out of bed and walked toward the bathroom. "I'm going to shower. You can go now. I'll be fine."

"Okay, I have something to do, and then I'll come back and take you to dinner."

"It's not necessary."

"Does that mean you don't want to see me tonight?"

"You know that's not true." She moved closer to him, until their bodies almost touched. "Aren't your parents coming soon?"

"Yes."

"Then you'd better get ready for their visit."

"I have a neighbor lady who cleans the house for me. She did that yesterday. All I need is to put flowers in their room for Mom."

* * *

She put her hands on his warm chest and looked into his eyes. "You're a nice man." His dimples showed when he smiled, which made him more handsome.

"When a woman says you're nice, it's usually the kiss of death for a relationship."

"Sometimes it just means you're nice." She kissed his cheek and rushed into the bathroom, firmly shutting the door between them. Kat leaned against it as her heartbeat raced, feeling the flush heat her cheeks. *Damn, I'm falling in love with him.* She heard him whistling as he left her room.

He hollered, "I'll lock your door and be back in a few hours."

In the shower, she considered her situation as the

cold water cascaded over her hot body. *I have a lot of thinking to do. If I want to change my life, now is the time to decide what to do. But if I get asked back to my job as a detective, which I might when my papers regarding my dismissal go in front of my superior's boss, then I'll probably never change. I am happy and good at being a detective.* She closed her eyes and turned to let the water run over her soapy back. The sensation of tears on her cheeks surprised her.

"I haven't cried this much since that awful day."

CHAPTER 10

Madison called Scott. "Are you at the station?"

"No, actually, I'm not far from your address."

"Do you know how to get here?"

Scott laughed. "I know how to get everywhere around San Diego County. Why?"

"I want to talk to you. I'm home. Come on by."

I know I ought to wait and let my temper calm down, but I don't want to. Scott and Gavin made a mistake when Kat was eleven, and I plan to help them correct it.

He'd barely changed into shorts when the doorbell rang. Scott stood outside with a grin on his face. Madison yanked him inside and punched him in the jaw.

Lying on the floor, Scott growled, "What the hell got into you?"

"Hearing a story about an eleven-year-old who got attacked by some mean boys and the stupid brothers who let her convince them to not tell her parents." He yanked Scott up by his collar. "Now, start explaining before I hit you again."

"Damned if I'll let you hit me again." Scott threw a punch, and Madison blocked it and hit him, knocking him back on the floor.

"I'll get my brother, Cory, to beat you up."

Suddenly, Scott laughed, and so did Madison.

Madison held out his hand. "Get up and help me decide how we're going to correct past mistakes."

Scott touched his chin gingerly. "You pack a mean punch." He looked down at his feet. "I knew this was going to come up and bite us in the ass, one of these days." He glanced at Madison. "I'm surprised she told you."

"You want a beer or bourbon before we start discussing how to solve this problem?"

"Sure, a drink would be good. I think I'd like to sit outside. I see your patio. It's cool out today and might make my jaw quit hurting."

"Go ahead. I'll bring your drink out there and an ice pack for your jaw. Which do you want, beer or bourbon?"

Scott sighed deeply. "As this is going to be a serious conversation, I think I need the bourbon."

While Madison made the drinks, he considered Scott's reaction to his attack. *He's a good guy and wasn't a grown man when all this happened. Keeping it a secret has been wearing on him.* He grabbed a bag of chips, put ice in a towel, and then drinks on a tray, and walked outside.

"It's nice and peaceful here," Scott said. When he saw

the ice in the towel, he quickly relieved Madison of it. "My jaw's hurting."

"Good. You deserve it."

"You're right."

"Don't agree with me. I want to stay mad at you."

Scott grinned as best he could. "You like me. Stop being mad. I made a foolish mistake when I was young."

"It's affected your sister's life in many ways."

"I know. I've tried to keep Kat safe. I knew if she died on duty, Gavin and I would never get over it."

"Do you know what she wanted to do before all of this happened?"

"Not really. Kat liked to read, and I thought she'd follow in Mom and Deirdre's footsteps and be a teacher."

"Your parents need to know what happened, but she has to tell them. I believe only then will she realize what she really wants out of life. Feeling helpless convinced her that to be safe, she had to be as tough as her brothers."

"I've thought the same, but whenever I tried to talk about that time, Kat shut me right down and usually walked off. Same with Gavin. What do you suggest?"

"We three have to convince her to talk about the incident with your parents. She has to open up and let go of her anger and determination that she has to be as strong as humanly possible."

"Why are you so determined that she heals from her childhood experience?" Scott eyed him and took a long swallow of his bourbon drink.

"Good question. One reason, Kat needs to heal and

get past that bad memory. The other, I'm not certain, but I think I may be feeling more for Kat than I'd planned. After my divorce, I promised I'd steer clear of women." He shrugged. *I especially wanted to stay away from having sex with one and coming to like her more and more.*

"I guess I can understand. I've thankfully never been divorced. Mom and Dad were sad to see Kat's marriage fail."

"He sounds like a real jerk."

"My brothers and I thought so, but she didn't want to hear that from us."

"If we see him, point him out."

"Why?"

"I plan to punch him harder than I did you. He said some awful, hurtful things to your sister."

"We figured, but she kept a tight lip about her marriage around the family."

"I heard her thrashing around and talking in her sleep. I lay down beside her to give her comfort. She kept rambling about what happened to her as a kid in her sleep."

"Ah, I wondered if she'd tell you all of what happened. You listened."

"I did."

"Humph, how is she now?"

"Better. We're going out to dinner this evening."

"Maybe my brother and I ought to join you."

"No. Let her approach you in her own time."

"Yeah, I guess you're right." Scott finished his drink and stood. "I'll call in and say I don't feel well. I seldom take a sick day, but I don't want everyone at headquarters asking who punched me." He grinned and groaned. "It probably won't be gone by tomorrow."

Madison shook his head, no. "Tell them you and I got to teasing about who was the strongest, and you lost."

"Hell, no. I can think up a better story than yours."

They shook hands at the door, and Madison watched as Scott drove out of sight. He raked his hand through his hair.

Damn, I lied. There's no question about my feelings for her. I am falling in love with his sister.

* * *

The Police Commander had called and asked Kat to come in to see him. She'd tried to delay their meeting, but he insisted on seeing her today.

She viewed herself in the mirror. She'd decided on a dark suit and low heels. *I want to look professional. I haven't had time to choose between going back or returning to school and getting my counseling degree. Well, I'll see how I feel when the time comes to decide.*

The drive downtown was quicker than usual. It was past the rush hour for most commuters.

There were plenty of spaces to park at the station, so she chose one close to the entrance. Everyone she saw greeted her with a smile. The elevator was empty, and she arrived quickly on the top floor. The Commander's personal assistant, Annie, greeted her pleasantly.

"Have a seat. I'll let the Commander know you've arrived."

He came out to greet Kat and ushered her into his office. "You're looking good. How's the shoulder and arm?"

"Almost healed. I saw my doctor a few days ago. He said it's going to be fine."

"Let's sit over here in the comfortable chairs. I had Annie make us fresh coffee, and she got some donuts."

Kat sank down into the comfortable chair and reached for a donut. Her Commander filled her cup with coffee and then his own.

"Don't tell my wife I've been eating sugary food in the office." He patted his stomach. "I'm supposed to be on a diet." He slid back in his chair, took a bite and sipped his coffee.

"Annie makes better coffee than you," Kat said. She'd tasted his before.

"So many people have told me that I've delegated the coffee-making to her."

"Was she glad?"

"She didn't like mine either."

"I like talking with you, Sir, but I'm sure you didn't ask me here just to have coffee and donuts."

"Maybe I ought to do it more often, to get to know my men and women better."

"I'm certain you know everything that happens."

"Well, I hope so. I had gone out of the office for a few hours. I'm sure your supervisor knew that and had planned the time to fire you."

"Maybe I deserved it."

"You deserved a lecture and maybe a few days off without pay. You are too impetuous, and you put yourself in danger more than most of my men." He looked directly at her. "Want to tell me why?"

Kat bit the edge of her lip. "Not right now. I need to talk first with my parents, but I'm not certain whether I want to come back to the police force."

Her Commander studied her carefully. "Okay, but the offer is open until you give me a definite no."

"Thank you for your support and understanding."

"You know, your father taught me a lot before he retired."

"I hope you aren't doing this for me because of my father. If I come back, I want to do it on my own terms."

"No, I'm not. You know your supervisor is a relative of mine. I was encouraged when the opening came up to give him the opportunity. He'd been a Detective for some time, so I reluctantly agreed. As I feared, he let the position go to his head. He was demoted, not only because of how he handled you, but also I'd had other complaints and had been keeping an eye on his work.

"You're a darn good detective and have good instincts. I do wish you'd be more careful of your own well-being."

They stood, and she shook his hand. "I won't keep you waiting too long for my decision. But I want to wait until after Christmas Day to talk with my family."

"That's soon. Have you got all your shopping done?"

"Some of it. When I leave here, I'm heading to the stores to finish up."

"Have a happy holiday and tell your parents hello."

* * *

Kat got in her car and sat staring out the windshield. *Maybe I won't wait. I'll go talk to Mom and Dad, if he's around. I won't know for sure what I want until this is out in the open.* Taking a deep breath, she started the car and headed for her parents' house.

Her Dad waved as she parked her car. He was cutting the lawn. They'd tried to get him to hire someone to do that chore, but he'd resisted. Working on the grass and shrubbery was not a chore to him. He turned off the lawnmower and walked toward her.

"I was just thinking about going in and having a cold drink of Mom's tea. How about you?"

"I'd love a tall glass of iced tea."

"With lots of ice, I know," he said and grinned. "Go on in and find out what your mother is up to."

"I will." Kat took a deep breath to calm herself. It helped little. She looked in the family room, but it was empty. Her Mom was in her bedroom, dusting.

"What a surprise," Mom said and walked across the room to hug her daughter gently. "How's your injury?"

"Much better. I think I'll be released to work after I see my doctor in two weeks. If I still have a job to return to, that is. The Commander called me in today and offered me my job back."

"That's wonderful."

"I'm not sure I want to go back."

Her Dad had walked to the door and stood holding two glasses of tea. "I brought your drinks here in case you want to talk in private."

"No, Dad. I have something I must tell you and Mom. I'd planned to wait until after Christmas, but I need to get it out while I still have the courage."

Her parents looked at her with concern in their eyes. "It's about whatever changed you when you were eleven," her Mom said.

Kat's throat tightened. She nodded.

"Then let's go sit where we'll be comfortable, and you can tell us whatever is bothering you," her Dad said. Then he leaned down and looked straight into her eyes. "But you know whatever it is won't change our feelings for you."

Tears pooled in her eyes, and she blinked, trying not to cry. "I know you love us all unconditionally. I didn't realize how many of my friends didn't have that security until they told me how much they liked you two."

Her father shepherded them out and into the family room. Kat sat in the soft recliner in front of the fireplace, and they pulled up chairs to face her. "Now, you are safe. Tell us whatever it is troubling you," her Dad said and kissed her forehead. Her Mom took hold of her hand.

She told them about the boys harassing her and touching her inappropriately, and about how Scott and Gavin rescued her. Her father opened his mouth to speak, and she put up her hand. "I made them promise they wouldn't tell you or Mom. I begged, cried and threatened to run away, and to tell all their secrets to Dad."

"Still," her mother said quietly. "It was their duty to come to us. I know they were only thirteen and sixteen and it wasn't as easy to talk about as now with the woman's movement. I'm sure they didn't know what to do and feared you would run away. I'm also certain they've regretted that decision to this day. They are especially protective of you. I thought it was because of your job, but it was much more.

"That's why you insisted I teach you how to fight and shoot. All the same training as your brothers," her Dad said.

"Yes. I was determined to be able to protect myself. I've never even told Scott and Gavin, but years later, when I was in my first year of college, those same boys cornered me as I left the bar where my friends and I hung out. We never drank much, but it was a happy place to meet with good music. We liked to go there after a hard test.

"Anyway, those guys cornered me beside my car. It was dark, and no one else was around." Kat smiled at her Dad. "You taught me well. They were stunned at how fast I managed to kick, hit, and have them on the ground." For a second, Kat remembered the feeling of satisfaction that rushed through her veins. And how her heart raced. "I jumped in my car and drove off."

"Did they ever approach you again?" her Dad asked.

"No. Afterwards, if they saw me in the hallway, they'd walk on the other side."

"I'm still going to have a conversation with Scott and Gavin, but it's Christmas time. I'll wait until after the holidays. Don't tell them you've talked with us, or they'll worry," he said.

"No problem. I want everyone to be in good spirits.

Madison and his family are coming for dinner," her Mom added.

"That's why I wanted to wait to tell you two, but I have to make a decision about going back to my job or doing something different. Now that everyone important will know, I can breathe again." Kat straightened her shoulders. "I feel like a weight has lifted off me."

"Do you think you'll go back to the police force?" her father asked.

"I have no idea. There are lots of things to think about. I considered going back to school to get my master's degree in counseling. It's a big decision."

"Whatever you decide is all right with us," her father said as he stood. "You'll be good at either job." He patted her head as he walked by, just like he used to when she was little. "I'm going to finish the yard. You two keep visiting."

"I feel like such an awful mother. Why didn't I suspect something?"

"Because I'm a good actress, even at eleven."

Her mother laughed. "You're trying to make me feel better."

Kat turned and took her Mom's hand. "You and Dad are the best parents anyone could have. We were loved, scolded when necessary, and sent to our rooms. We knew our limits. We felt safe." She put up her hand when her mother started to speak. "You are the best. Accept it, or I won't come to Christmas dinner."

Her Mom laughed. "That's a lie. You'd never miss my turkey and dressing or the mincemeat pie I make especially for you."

"I know you're right. I can't even find that kind of pie in any store. But yours is the best anyway."

"And I expect you are looking forward to seeing your SEAL again."

"He's not *my* SEAL, Mom."

"You must not lie to your mother."

Kat raised her shoulders and sighed. "If you must know, I am beginning to like him more than I want to."

"He'd be a perfect match for you."

"How so?"

"I suspect you are both loners. Somehow, I got that impression about him when we were together. You'll be happy to be together when he's home, and you can have your own time when he's away."

"What about his private time?"

Her Mom chuckled. "I expect he's quite able to figure that out for himself. You both may like having your quiet time together."

Kat shook her head. "You amaze me, Mom."

"Good."

Kat left shortly afterward and headed to her condo. Tiredness had her shoulders slumping. Getting it all out had eased her conscience. But was she any closer to deciding what to do with her life?

When she locked her car to go upstairs, part of her hoped to see Madison's vehicle parked nearby. She didn't see it anywhere. Inside, she kicked off her shoes and headed to the kitchen for a glass of wine and some nuts to snack on. Her phone rang as she poured the Riesling into her wine glass. She took a sip and answered.

"Hi," Madison said. "I'm running late. My parents surprised me and flew in early. I thought the four of us might go to eat at the restaurant where we met."

"Actually, we met at the hospital. You were a bit dopey at the time and called me an Amazon."

"Admit it, you liked my nickname."

"Never," she said and chuckled.

"Are you all right with my plans?"

Kat bit her lip. She hadn't prepared herself to meet his parents before Christmas Day, but this might be the best idea.

"I'm waiting patiently," Madison said into the phone.

"I'd like to meet your parents before our crowded Christmas dinner. Can we go a bit later, say seven-thirty? Or is that too late for your parents?"

"No, they'll be fine. We're having a drink with some hors d'oeuvres, and then they'll want to rest and unpack."

"Great. I'm a bit tired myself, so I'll relax, too. See you later."

When she put down the phone, she went back into her living room and sat, letting her mind wander while she sipped her drink. *Today emotionally exhausted me. I wanted to call off eating out, but I am curious to meet Madison's parents and see their reaction to me. My ex-husband's parents never were too fond of me. I imagine they were glad to see us divorce. Before I let my feelings get too tangled up in Madison, I'd best meet his parents and note their reaction.*

Too tired to finish her snack and drink, she went into her bedroom and lay across the bed and went right to sleep.

When the doorbell rang, she woke feeling groggy. *Damn, that's probably them.* The bell rang again. Kat sat on the edge of her bed and waited to get more awake before heading to the door. There was nothing to do but admit she'd slept past the time to get ready.

"I thought something had happened when you didn't call out or anything," Madison said, looking her up and down. Behind him, a man who was obviously his father smiled. His petite wife moved around her son.

"I'm Terry Carney. Please don't be embarrassed. You obviously were sleeping. Are you feeling well?"

Madison grinned. "That's my mother. The nurse in her comes out very easily."

"No, I was tired, but never expected to sleep this long. Please, come in. I'm so sorry I'm not ready. Why don't you all go on without me? Knowing Madison, I'm sure he's made reservations."

"I can call and move them out an hour. Get dressed. We'll wait."

"I-"

"No protests. Get going. We're a patient family."

Kat had to smile. "Wait until you meet mine. Not so patient, but I love them. Okay, I'll hurry."

* * *

Madison watched his mother walk around Kat's living room.

"I like the way she's decorated this room. Warm colors that are both welcoming and relaxing." She stopped in front of pictures spread in a diamond-shaped arrangement. "I gather this is her family."

Madison stood behind her to look at the photos, and his Dad looked over her other shoulder. "Yes. I haven't met them all, but I know Scott and this must be his wife and three boys. The one at the bottom is her youngest brother, Cory. He's just became a SEAL. He's doing well.

"Scott is a detective, and another brother is a firefighter. I don't know much about him. I know she and her sister are the only girls."

"We're anxious to meet them," his Dad said. "They sound like a great family, from what you've told us."

"And we suspect you might like Kat a bit more than any other woman you've dated since your divorce."

"Which have been few," Madison said.

"Just don't move too quickly. You want to find the one you'll stay married to for at least thirty years or more," his Dad said with a sparkle in his eyes when he looked at his wife. "We're headed toward forty."

"Mom and Dad, I've never asked, but was there a reason you only had me?"

His Mom sat on the couch. "We had two miscarriages before you were born and one after your birth. The doctor advised that for health reasons that we shouldn't try again. It was hard for me, mentally and physically. We were so thankful we had you, and we'd have had more children if possible. Did you feel lonely being the only one?"

"No. You were great parents and always had me involved in sports and all kinds of activities. The house was full of my friends most of the time."

"I'm glad. Would you want children, Madison?"

"Yes, Mom, but maybe not six."

"Ah," Kat said as she entered the room. "I see you've been looking at my large family."

Madison smiled at her. "That was fast."

"When you were one of six, you had to be fast to get the best piece of chicken or pie. It was great fun growing up. Shall we go?"

Madison opened the door and waved his hand. "Let's get some food." Kat was the last to pass by him. He leaned down and kissed the top of her head.

"What was that for?"

He shrugged. "Just because."

"Because?"

"Yeah." He lowered his voice. "Whenever I look at you and smell that sexy perfume, I have to move closer."

"Behave. Remember, I want to make a good impression on your parents, who are patiently waiting for us at the elevator."

He laughed and put his arm around her waist. "They are understanding and tolerant."

* * *

The restaurant was full, but the owner, who knew Madison and some of the other SEALs in his team, had saved them a quiet table in the back of the Wisteria Italian Restaurant.

Madison introduced Kat to Arnaldo Calabria.

"It is good to see your parents are visiting with you again. How have you been since your last trip, Randy?"

Mr. Calabria asked Madison's father. "I heard you'd had some heart surgery."

"Much better, and my son came home to help my wife. The two of them took good care of me."

"I got some news from your boss, Jackson, and his sweet wife, Kayla," the restaurateur told Madison. "They come in for dinner every chance they get. But I'd better get your orders before you starve."

After they ordered, the music started. Madison stood and held out his hand to Kat. She shook her head.

"Why not?"

"I'm terrible at dancing. I never learned how."

"The small floor is full. No one will notice."

His mother stood. "I'm going to dance," she said. "Especially since it's a nice slow number." Her husband pushed up from his chair and guided her to the dance floor.

"Come on," Madison said coaxingly. "It's fun."

And I'll probably make a fool of myself. I can't remember when I last attempted dancing. Kat put out her hand, and Madison gave her his sexy smile that made her heart race.

"Good girl." He led her onto the dance floor, pulled her close and moved slowly around in time with the music. She stepped on his toes.

"See. I'll have you limping."

His laugh rang out, and several people looked their way.

Kat hit his shoulder. "Stop. Now everyone is looking at us."

"Then let's give them a reason to look." He bent and

kissed her before she realized his intent. Kat's body naturally shifted closer to his.

His parents danced past them and his Dad said, "No kissing on the dance floor."

Both pulled away, and even Madison blushed, which he never did.

Kat had to laugh. "Payback," she teased.

Later, as they finished their meal and were enjoying coffee, Kat realized she hadn't had so much fun in a long time.

"Nickel for your thoughts," Madison whispered.

"You'd need much more money than a nickel."

"A dollar?"

"A million."

"Hah. You'll tell me eventually."

"No way. This has been a lovely evening. I'm so glad I got to meet you both before Christmas dinner," Kat said to the older Carneys.

"We are, too. Maddy told us a little about your family, but I understand he hasn't met all of them. We are pleased your mother invited us to Christmas dinner."

"I'm glad she did, too. You call Madison, Maddy?"

Terry laughed. "We named him after his grandfather, and all the family called him Maddy for short. I've gathered our son hasn't told his friends that nickname. They usually call him Doc or Professor."

"Mom, you've told Kat all my secrets about my name. I prefer Madison."

"Good, then I'll call you Maddy," Kat said and grinned.

He groaned. "See, Mom and Dad? Now everyone will know."

"It's a nice name," his mother protested.

"It sounds feminine."

"Well, we could call you Warrior, since Madison means son of a mighty warrior."

Madison groaned. "This is getting worse. Let's go."

On the way home, all three teased him until they got to Kat's condo. "I'm tired. I hope you don't mind if I don't invite you up. I need to get my sleep. I'll be doing last minute shopping with the crazy crowds tomorrow to get a few more presents. I'll see you on Christmas Day."

Madison frowned, and she laughed. "It was really nice meeting you first before my family takes over." She kissed his Mom and Dad on the cheek and then waved and disappeared inside the condo's main door.

"I like her," his Dad said.

"I do, too. Kathleen will make a good wife for you."

"Mom and Dad, we're both divorced and not looking to marry anyone anytime soon."

"That's what all of men say, just before we're suddenly standing in front of the preacher," his Dad said and kissed his Mom before she could reply.

"We aren't in a hurry."

"You better be if you want children. Neither one of you is getting any younger," his Mom noted.

Madison gave up, smiled, and drove home.

CHAPTER 11

They didn't see Kat again until they arrived at her parents' home. Madison drove, since he'd been there before. The yard and outside of the house were decorated. Several young children ran around the lawn decorations, laughing and yelling. When Madison helped his mother out of the car, he noticed she had tears in her eyes.

"What's wrong, Mom?"

"This is the way Christmas should be. I sometimes feel sad for the babies I lost and the ones I couldn't have."

"I didn't want to make you unhappy. We can go and do Christmas on our own."

His mother blinked. "Don't you dare. I'm looking forward to all this fun."

Just then, Brody and Lil Cafferty walked out to greet them. Madison stood and watched his parents. He'd never known how much they'd wanted a larger family, and he realized he was looking forward to spending a different kind of Christmas with them.

"Please come in the house. I've threatened my grown children to sit quietly for a minute so I can introduce you," Mr. Cafferty said with a wide smile. "Christmas is usually a bit crazy around here. Once we get back from church, it's a free-for-all." He motioned for the Carneys to enter in front of him and his wife.

Kat stood by the doorway into the living room. Fragrant aromas from the kitchen filled the air.

"It smells so good it already makes me hungry," Terry Carney said to her hostess.

Cory got up and walked across the room. Madison turned to his parents. "Mom and Dad, this is Cory. He's the SEAL I told you about."

"I still get shivers when I hear someone say I'm a SEAL. It seems unreal at times."

"You'll get over that in a few months," Madison said. "Except once in a while, something happens and you feel that thrill again."

"Nice to know."

Kat introduced the Carneys to her family, except the children playing outside. When she got to Scott, she frowned. "How did you get a black eye?"

"I punched him," Madison said.

Scott grinned at Madison and made light of it. "Not really. I stopped by your boyfriend's house and stumbled on the way out to the pool area."

"I don't remember any place that might cause you to stumble. I went there to question Madison after his car almost got stolen and I had no difficulty walking around."

"Oh, hell. Shall I tell her the truth, Madison? Otherwise she'll wear me down with questions all day."

"I'll explain to her later."

Kat stomped her foot. "I want to know now!"

Scott laughed. "This is the real side of my sister. Any sweetness she's shown you is an act. We called her the Grumpy Bear Sister." He motioned to Deirdre, coming out of the kitchen and depositing a bowl on the table. "She's the sweet one." Then he pulled Kat into his arms. "Not that we don't love Grumpy Bear, but be warned — she's a handful."

Madison glanced at his parents, who appeared to enjoy listening to their conversation. He took hold of Kat's arm and whispered, "Let's go outside where the children aren't playing."

"Why?"

"I thought you wanted your answer."

"Something's going on here. All right, I imagine we've embarrassed your parents enough."

"Don't go for our sake. We haven't had this much fun in a long time," Terry Carney said.

But Madison put his arm around Kat and led her outside and around the side of the house, away from the children. "We can talk here. That way, if you get upset, I can handle you."

She tipped her head up to his, and he smiled. She did it more than she realized.

"What's so funny?"

Madison bent and kissed her chin. "You pointed

your chin upward as though to dare anyone to touch you."

"Maybe I'm warning you."

"I'm not afraid of you."

She kicked him in the shin.

"Ah, now you have to suffer the consequences." He pulled her tight against him and kissed her.

For a second, she leaned into him, and he deepened his kiss. Then, out of the blue, she shoved him. He almost fell, but got his balance. Then he stalked her as she moved backward.

"That wasn't nice. I enjoyed every second. Didn't you?"

"Yes, but I don't want you to think you can grab me anytime you want."

"Have I done that?"

She lowered her head and mumbled no.

"I can't hear you."

Kat moved further back and raised her head. "We came out here to discuss how my brother got his black eye and bruised face."

"You are very observant. The bruises are almost gone. If you really must know, I punched Scott in the face." Madison bit his lip to keep from smiling at her startled expression.

"Why would you do such a thing?"

He smoothed his hand across her forehead. "You're going to get wrinkles if you frown so much."

"Why?" she asked again.

"Because he and your brother didn't tell your

parents about what happened to you as a child. They were old enough to know better."

"I recently told my parents."

"Good. How did your Mom and Dad take hearing the information years after it happened?"

"Wonderful, of course. Mom and Dad both expressed concern that they hadn't understood why I changed so much. I think I got them to accept it was in no way their fault."

He pulled her close and put his chin on her head. "If anyone ever hurts you again, they'll regret it forever."

* * *

She moved slightly and tipped her head up. Her heart raced, and every nerve in her body reacted to where Madison touched her. She'd never been so aware of a man as she was of him.

"Are you for real?" she asked.

"Yes, and I think I may be falling in love with you, including the grumpy side."

"You mustn't say that, not now."

"Why?"

"It's too soon. We both made mistakes before."

"I didn't feel this way with my first wife."

Kat snuggled her head into his shoulder. *What can I say? That I feel different around him, more than I ever did with my husband? I'm afraid of being a failure in marriage again. This time, with Madison, I expect it would devastate me much more than the first divorce did.*

He leaned closer and tried to look at her face. "Are you all right?"

"Just scared."

His chuckle vibrated in his chest, where her cheek lay against him. Kat glanced up. "Aren't you?"

"You mean, scared?"

Her eyes met his. "Yes."

"Holding you in my arms feels right, but I understand we both need to take some time and be sure."

"Thank goodness," she whispered. When she pulled back, he let her go.

Her mother called out the screen door, "Christmas dinner is ready."

"We'll talk later," he said as they walked inside.

"Give it a few days."

"All right. I'll wait until Mom and Dad leave. How's that?"

"Fine. Now, I'm hungry. Stop talking so much." She looked over her shoulder and winked at him.

The rest of the day went well. Madison noted how Kat's parents and his folks seemed to get along well. Her brothers, sister and sisters-in-law loved to tease each other, and the happy spirit continued until it was time to take all the tired children home.

When Gavin came to say goodbye, he grinned at Madison. "I understand I have a punch coming to me."

"Don't worry. I think your brother got all the heat of my anger."

"Well, if you want to hit me, I'll take it. We were wrong, but we were still kids. Having her save us from a reaming out by our father sounded good at the time, but the main reason we stayed quiet was because we were afraid she'd do something drastic, like running away, if we told. We love her, and we didn't know what to do."

Gavin put out his hand. "Friends?"

"Sure."

"By the way, Madison is a long name. Didn't your team give you a nickname we can use?"

"Not really."

"Then," Gavin raised his voice, getting everyone's attention, "From now on, this is Maddy."

"No!"

"Yes!" The chorus came from more than just his parents.

"This really makes you part of the family," Gavin told him.

"I may punch you out anyway."

Laughing, Gavin and his family took their leave.

"Are you two ready to go?" Madison asked his parents. "I don't want Dad to get too tired."

"I've had a wonderful time, but I guess it is a good time to leave."

Kat's parents hugged his and spoke of meeting for lunch before the Carneys left town.

"I'll drop you off first," he told Kat on the way to his car. "You look as tired as my parents. I guess with so much happening to you these last few days, it's been exhausting."

"It has."

He pulled into her condo's parking area and went up the elevator with her to walk her to her door. There, he cupped her face in his palm and kissed her. "Sleep tight."

He'd just reached the door to the stairs when she called, "Sleep tight, Maddy." Then she quickly shut and locked her door.

Madison heard her laughter on the other side. "I'll get back at you, just wait," he called out before taking the steps down two at a time. He'd always preferred stairs to elevators.

* * *

Madison called Kat several times to invite her to join him and his parents on trips around town, but she had an excuse each day.

"I wish you had gotten a chance to know Kat better before you had to leave," he said to his parents as he drove them to the airport.

"Maybe she needs some time and space before seeing you again," his Mom said. "I like her, and I think she's sensible wanting to slow things down between you two."

"Yeah, she's right. We both made mistakes the first time we got married. He dropped his parents in front of the airport entrance. "I'll park and come with you to security."

"Don't," his Dad said, leaning in the car window. "We have plenty of help here. You need to get back to work."

"Are you sure?"

"Positive. Go on. Plan on visiting us in a few months."

"Let me know what the doctor says when you see him."

"He'll say I'm fine. Go on."

Madison waited until they entered the airport and then drove toward the base. If he managed to get off early, he might convince Kat to come to his house for a barbecue tonight.

When he entered the control room, he saw his teammates were crowded around the planning desk. Several maps had been spread out.

"Glad you got here," Captain Buchanan said. "We have a mission coming up. I want you all to be aware of the territory and the necessity to move in and get out fast." He pointed to several spots on the map. "You'll be flown in at night and parachute into this area. It has some coverage from trees and hills, and if you parachute in tomorrow night, there'll be little moonlight."

"What's our target?" Ranger asked.

"A rogue group has captured an American woman. They want a million dollars for her safe return. They sent the Ambassador a picture of her." He flashed the picture up on the wall screen. Buchanan glanced at his men. "She's young, eighteen, and from the looks of her face, they aren't being gentle with her."

"Damn," Heath said. "I can't wait to get my hands on the men who hurt her."

"Then go home, take care of what you need to do. We leave at daybreak."

"Why not sooner, Captain?" Heath asked.

"I expect they are trying to do some behind-the-scenes talking first."

Ranger swore. "Damn fools. These guys want

money. They're wasting our time. We need to leave now."

Captain Buchanan snapped, "Lower your voice unless you want to be demoted and thrown off this team."

Ranger glanced around. "Is the Commander nearby?"

"Yes, and he agreed with you, but to no avail."

"I'm out of here," Ranger said. "We report at dawn?"

Buchanan nodded. "Right. Madison, stay back."

"Yes, Sir."

"You don't have a wife at home. Stay here with me, and we'll see what other info gets sent to us. We need a good plan ready to go when we hit the ground."

Well, there goes my idea of a barbecue. Just as well. By the time I get back, we'll have a better idea of whether to go forward with our relationship.

Madison looked out the window at the moon and turned back to the Captain.

"Where do we start?"

* * *

They were flying toward the Middle East as the sun rose. The whole team went over the plans again and again. There was one chance to free the hostage and get her home safe and sound.

Later, while several of his teammates slept, Madison closed his eyes and went back over everything in his mind. Rescue operations were more intense. Not only were their lives on the line, but so were the lives of any hostages. He felt the bench give as one of the guys sat beside him. Looking through slitted eyes, he saw Cory.

Cory whispered, "Kat asked me to give you this letter. I have no idea what's in it."

"Is she going back to work for the police?"

"I think so, but she seems to be in a better frame of mind. Maybe she won't be too risky with her life."

Madison chuckled. "You're kidding, right?"

"Not really. Kat promised Mom and Dad she would be more cautious."

"I hope so."

"Anyway, she asked me to see you got this letter."

After Cory handed the envelope to Madison, he walked over to the cooler for a bottle of water and then lay down on a nearby bench and closed his eyes.

Madison moved the letter around in his hands. He caught a whiff of her perfume and studied her handwriting. Like her, it was straight and firm. He smiled at his thoughts.

Maybe I ought to wait and read it on the way back. I don't need any distractions now or I can tear it up. Whatever she has to say, I'd rather hear it face to face.

Bending down, he slipped it into his duffel bag and with no one watching tore it into small pieces. *In person will be a better way to hear what she has to say. It might have been a goodbye letter, or I like you a lot, but let's be friends ...* He grinned, picturing her in his mind, and then he deliberately turned his thoughts to the mission and shut out everything else.

* * *

They parachuted into enemy territory five miles from the encampment where intelligence had it the young woman was being held. The ambassador had no luck with negotiations, and the kidnappers threatened to behead her in two days if they hadn't received the ransom they'd demanded. All the team members were aware they had one chance for success.

Once landed, they quickly rolled up their chutes and hid them. One by one, the team started walking toward the target area.

Heath swatted a mosquito and swore softly. The Team's least favorite setting was trekking through a mosquito-infested area. Their spray helped some, but not completely.

When they got close, they smelled the campfire and heard men's voices, talking and laughing. The captive still tied to the post had her head down. Bear put up his hand and motioned for Kijika and Madison to join him.

"Get as close as you can. Check for the number of men and see if you can hear what they're planning. Madison you can tell Kijika and he'll let me know."

"Right." Kijika and Madison got close to the ground and moved out of sight. The rest of the team sat to wait with guns ready.

* * *

Kijika inched closer to the kidnappers. He gasped when he saw the young woman tied to a post near the fire. She was naked and had several burn marks on her shoulders and belly. Her head hung down and tears ran down her face.

"Are we going to give her back when we get the money?" one man standing next to a tall, lean man, asked.

"Hell no. We'll sell the bitch to someone overseas who likes pretty young ladies."

Madison whispered through his mouthpiece to Kijika about what he'd heard.

The hostage looked up. She snarled and spit at the two men near her. The tall man backhanded her, but she didn't cry out. Then the man put his hands around her neck and Kijika saw his fingers flex in a squeeze.

Madison scooted backward and he contacted Bear to tell him.

"Shoot him before he kills her. We'll be right behind you."

"Right." Madison relayed Bear's message to Kijika and they moved as close as possible without the kidnappers seeing them. The woman's face had turned a dark red. Madison and Kijika's bullets hit the two men standing beside her in the chest, and they took out several others before the kidnappers had a chance to grab their rifles.

Their team ran past them, bullets flying, as they entered the camp. Kijika shot a man who was pointing his rifle toward the captive. Madison rushed to her side and cut the ropes. Taking her in his arms, he carried the young woman out of camp.

"I'll be right back," he hollered to Kijika. But when he

ran back to help, his teammates had wiped out most of the group and secured the few survivors.

"Let's get these guys up and make them run with us. Keep your guns against their backs. We'd better hurry to the boats. If they have friends nearby, they've heard the shots," Bear said. He radioed that they had freed the hostage and were on their way to the shore with their few prisoners.

Kijika had found a blanket and wrapped the young woman in it. Then he carried her as he ran with the others. Two boats arrived at the same time they got to the creek. The team recovered their parachutes from where they'd hid them in the bushes and threw them onto the boat. The prisoners were told to sit on the floor.

Bear, Madison, Heath and Ranger shot at the men, who suddenly emerged from the forest, killing several.

"They did have friends not far off. We were lucky," Ranger said as the wind rushed across his face. The boats left a high wake as they moved quickly down the creek and out into the open ocean. When they arrived beside the larger boat waiting to take them on, the woman was moved first, and then the prisoners with the SEALs following.

Captain Buchanan greeted them with a huge grin. "Looks like the plan went perfectly." He clapped several men on the back and shook the hands of others. The prisoners sat on the deck and frowned at the group.

One of them said, "Our men will find us, and then you'll see how fierce we can fight." He spat at Ranger's boot. Ranger pretended to slip, letting the toe of his shoe kick the prisoner in the side.

"They won't find you in the United States military jail," Ranger said. The man gave him a fierce look and turned his head away.

Ranger walked to Madison's side. "How's our rescued lady doing?"

"Some of the wounds are deep. I gave her a shot so she'd sleep while I cleaned her injuries. I've also given her a shot of antibiotics. She's dirty and it would be too easy for her wounds to become infected."

"They mistreated her." Bear had walked up behind them.

"Yes, and at eighteen, I'm not sure how you mentally recover."

"With a lot of love and counseling," Bear said. "I asked the Captain to radio ahead that we have her safe, but she's in bad shape. Have to prepare her father for what he will see."

"If it was my daughter, I'd never rest until this entire group was annihilated," Madison said.

Ranger raised his eyebrows. "Wow, you never talk that way."

"I know, but the torture of this young woman makes me furious. Kijika told me how brave she was and that she spit in one man's face. The one Kijika thought was the leader."

"Then her strength will get her through this, with the proper care. Hopefully, her parents will be able to help her."

"I heard her mother hated this place and left six

months ago. The daughter wouldn't leave her father alone," the Captain said as he joined the group.

Heath smiled. "We need to name her Warrior Woman."

"That's a good title and might make her smile." Madison knelt back down and continued to clean her up as much as possible.

"I sure hope you have a good Dad and Mom," he whispered in her ear as he worked on her.

From base camp they flew her to the the main airport in that area. An ambulance was waiting when they landed, along with the Ambassador.

For her safety only Captain Buchanan and the higher ranked officers knew her father was the Ambassador. They'd kept her last name unknown.

Captain Buchanan got off the plane first and quickly walked to meet him. After speaking for a few minutes, he motioned for Madison to carry the rescued woman down the steps with Ranger's help. The ambulance personnel had brought a stretcher to the side of the plane. Her father and the Captain stood nearby.

Madison had let up on the pain medicine, so she'd be alert enough to see her whoever met her and know she was safe. As he carried her, she said, "Thank you all for saving my life. I don't think I'd have survived much longer. I wanted to give them as much of a fight and trouble as I could before they killed me. I'll pray for you and your team's safety."

Tears were in her eyes as Madison leaned down and said, "You are one of the bravest women our team has rescued. Never forget that." He placed her gently on the stretcher.

On the plane going home, Cory sat beside him. Madison smiled. "You did well. I saw you in the middle of the fight."

"You did better with the way you took care of our victim. I saw her bravery, too. I think if you and Kat ever get together, you'd have a daughter with her strength." Then he grinned. "I can't wait to watch more of your courtship."

"Courtship is an old-fashioned word."

"But it fits you and Kat. Wait and see." Cory left him to take a beer out of the tub of ice, crack it open and salute Madison.

CHAPTER 12

Kat looked down at her living room rug. *I've almost worn a hole in it from all the walking back and forth I've done this week. I need to make a final decision, although nothing about a job requires a final, forever decision. People change jobs all the time. But not my family.*

She sat on the sofa and closed her eyes. Did she want to go back to school and get her degree in counseling or settle back into her detective slot? Yesterday, when she'd talked on the phone to her Commander, he promised Marcos would be her partner.

Kat jumped up and grabbed her cellphone. "Hell, I've been dithering for days, when deep inside I've known my decision. I love being a detective. I'll try and be more careful, not as reckless."

She called the police station. When the Commander heard her decision, he chuckled. "I was almost sure you'd come back. You'd have disappointed Marcos and me if you decided otherwise.

"I told him if you returned, you'd be partners again.

Not that he doesn't think his present partner is doing fine, but the two of you are used to each other. I understand.

"It hasn't been that many years since I was working with my own favorite colleague," the Commander said. "Harry retired after I got promoted. He said the wife wanted to travel, and after all the years we worked together, he didn't think he'd work as well with a new person."

"I remember your partner on the beat. Dad said he and his wife travel a lot. Mom's been trying to get Dad to buy a motorhome and visit all the places they haven't seen."

"Is she having any luck?"

"She's wearing him down."

He laughed. "Wives know how to do that. I'll expect you in on Monday."

"I'll be there. I'm all healed."

When Kat put down the phone, her hand hesitated over it. *I have Maddy's number.* She liked the nickname instead of the more formal Madison. *I doubt he's back. We haven't heard from Cory. Maybe it's for the best that I forget Maddy and concentrate on my work. I'll go see my parents and tell them my decision.*

She'd barely gotten in the door of her parents' house before her mother said, "Cory called. He's back and fine. All the guys are going to celebrate at someplace called Aces Bar and Grill tonight. He'll come by and see us tomorrow. They've been given a long weekend off."

"I'm glad he's back safe. Did he say if anyone on his team had been hurt?"

"No, but I doubt he'd have been in such good spirits if one of them was injured." Her mother raised her eyebrows. "Are you thinking of anyone in particular?"

"Well, I did wonder about Madison."

"I'd assume he's well. Why don't you get a girlfriend to go with you tonight and check out if he's at Aces?"

"I think someone mentioned he doesn't usually go there the first night. He likes to be at home."

"You might ask your brother."

"No, it's not important. I came to tell you I'm starting back to work on Monday." She studied her mother's face. "You don't seem surprised."

"I'm not. I know police work is in your blood, just like it's in your brother's. But I worry about your recklessness at times."

"I will be more careful. I promise."

"Good." Her Mom hugged her. "Do it for your Dad and me, if for no other reason. I baked today. Let's make tea and enjoy a piece of chocolate cake."

"Ah, Dad's favorite. I bet he's already had at least one piece, if not two."

"No bet."

"Where is he?"

"He drove to the men's toy store."

"Ah, the hardware store, but you love to call it the men's toy store."

"He tries to pretend he doesn't like the name, but I caught him once, smiling behind my back."

They'd just finished the tea and cake when the doorbell rang. "I wonder who that might be," her mother said. "We aren't expecting company."

"I'll get it on my way out." Kat volunteered. She opened the door and saw two police officers. Her heart sank. From their expressions, they were not bringing good news. "What's happened?" she asked in a shaky voice.

They introduced themselves and asked her relationship to Brody Cafferty. The older officer said, "A driver ran a red light. Your Dad's car was hit. He's at the hospital."

"Is he alive?"

"Yes, but he's injured. We'll drive you and Mrs. Cafferty there."

Her mother stepped up behind her. "Who is it?" And then she saw the police officers.

Kat repeated what they'd told her. "We need to let them get us to Dad quickly." Kat grabbed her Mom's jacket from the coat rack, and they rushed to get into the police car. Her mother held Kat's hand tight as they sped down the streets.

At the hospital, Kat held her Mom's arm as they walked into the emergency room. She was shaking and pale. They approached the admissions nurse. "Do you have Brody Cafferty here as a patient?" Kat asked.

"He's in surgery. Go up to the third floor and turn right. You can let the nurse know you're there and sit in the waiting room."

"Thank you. Do you have a wheelchair for my mother? She's shaking, and I'm afraid she might fall."

Another nurse overheard Kat and offered, "I'll get one and go with you upstairs. Give me a minute."

On the elevator, the nurse explained she knew who

Kat's father was and wanted to help them as much as possible.

Kat's mother raised her head. "How do you know my husband?"

"My brother got into trouble when he was younger," the woman explained. "Chief Cafferty took an interest in him, brought my brother into the local police station. He showed him around and then kept in touch with him until he finished school and got his four-year degree. Afterward, my brother joined the police department. He's been a police officer for almost fifteen years."

Kat's mother smiled sadly. "My husband is a good man. He helped many young men over the years while he was chief. He lost a few who kept up their criminal ways, but the others became police officers, teachers, and one even a lawyer."

The elevator opened on the third floor. The nurse took them to the waiting room and told the nurses at the station who they were.

She joined them in the waiting room. "The nurses will let the doctor know you're here. He'll come out and talk with you after the surgery."

Kat's mother put out her hand. "Bless you, my nerves are calmer now."

"I'm glad. I have to run, but I'll check on you later."

Kat took hold of her mother's hand when the nurse left. "Dad's a fighter, Mom. He'll fight for his life."

"I know. Will you call your brothers and sister. I'm too nervous to talk to all of them."

"I will." Kat used her cellphone to connect with her siblings in a group call—all but Cory, who she'd removed from the family ring due to his job. It took a while to explain what had happened to Dad, and they all told her they were on their way to the hospital. Then she called Cory.

"Hi, Sis. What's up? Are you going to join us this evening?"

"No, Dad's been in an accident. He's in surgery." She explained what had happened and where they were. "But you don't have to come if you're working. This waiting room will be full soon."

"Of course I'm coming. I'm at the base, though, so it'll take a little longer for me to get there."

"Be careful driving. See you whenever you arrive." She hung up and joined her Mom. "I guess you heard. The army of Caffertys will be here in no time."

Her mother patted her hand. "Thank goodness you were with me. I don't know what I'd have done."

"You'd have done fine. Dad was a cop before he got to Chief. He had a dangerous job for years."

"Yes, and just when I relaxed, he got hurt."

Kat was out of words. She sat by her mother and held her hand tight.

As she expected, her sister and older brothers arrived quickly, Scott and Gavin in the lead.

"I went by the fire station and got him," Scott explained. "The wives will come later. We knew it'd crowd the waiting room. They're always too small."

Deirdre was the next to arrive. She hurried to their mother's side and hugged her. Kat moved away to talk with their brothers.

"I'm surprised Lloyd isn't here yet," Scott said.

"He called. He's busy with a patient who's not doing well. He'll get here as soon as he can."

"Did you call Cory?" Gavin asked.

"Yes. He was on base, but he's on his way."

"How bad is it?" Scott whispered.

"Not good," Kat said. "From what we've been told, he's badly injured. I suspect he was bleeding internally, since they took him into surgery so quickly."

"Damn. He's enjoying his retirement so much, and Mom almost had him convinced to start traveling." Scott glanced at his Mom and Deirdre. "She always calmed Mom better than the rest of us."

"Yeah, I was glad to see her arrive and take over. I did okay, but not as good as Deirdre."

Her brothers both hugged her. "You did great. I'm so glad you were with Mom," Gavin said and kissed Kat's forehead.

Kat paced the hallways. Her brothers took turns joining her. Right now, Scott was her companion.

"I don't know what our family would do without Dad," Scott said.

"It'll happen sometime, but hopefully not soon. Dad and Mom aren't that old, and I know she hoped to get him to travel with her."

"Yeah, I caught him looking at RVs when I stopped in for a visit a few weeks before Christmas."

"She is wearing him down." Kat smiled at the picture in her head of their parents waving goodbye as they took off in an RV. "Let's hope they get to live that dream."

Just then, a tired-looking man in surgical scrubs

appeared at the doors leading to the operating rooms. Kat glanced at her watch. It had been five hours.

"I expect you two are part of Chief Cafferty's family. I'm the surgeon who took care of your Dad. Let's join the rest of your family. I'd rather talk to everyone at once."

Kat and Scott followed him into the waiting room. He walked straight to their mother and knelt to talk to her.

"Your husband had several areas that were bleeding, most from the spleen. We were able to save it. For now, all the bleeding is stopped. He's in recovery getting more blood, and from there, he'll go to the Intensive Care Unit. You'll hear us calling it the ICU.

"He's still in danger. As soon as he stabilizes, if he does, we'll have an orthopedic surgeon see him for his broken left arm. I'm surprised that's all he broke. The next seventy-two hours are important. If he doesn't bleed anymore, he'll have his arm fixed and go home a few days after that. But because of his age and the type of accident, we will watch him closely."

"Thank you, Doctor. I've been praying for him and you and your staff. I know you must be tired. I appreciate you taking the time to explain my husband's condition. We were lucky to have you take care of him after the accident."

"Just keep praying, and the staff and I will do our part to get him well." The doctor stood, shook hands, and answered a few more questions before leaving.

"At least Dad has a chance," Scott said. "He's a fighter."

Deirdre, ever the organized one, stepped forward with pen and paper. "One of us needs to be waiting in the visitors room for whenever they'll let one of us into ICU. Then when we have to leave the ICU, still sit the rest of the time waiting nearby to make sure a family member is available, whatever occurs."

"I can come in the evenings. Pamela can fill in for me if necessary," Scott said.

Kat moved forward. "I'll contact the Commander and see if I can delay coming back to work for at least a week. I'm sure he'll understand. As soon as I talk to him, I'll call you, Deirdre."

"Gavin, how about you?" Deirdre asked.

"I'm off the next few days. I'll take the overnight shift. I can sleep in the daytime."

Their mother stood up. "I intend to be here most of the time."

"No," her sons and daughters spoke at once.

Deirdre served as their spokesperson. "Mom, you have to rest. Dad will still need lots of care when he comes home."

"I still plan on coming to see him every day!"

"I'll come by after school's out and drive you here, but we won't stay long. You can see Dad, and then we're going home."

Cory looked torn. "I feel awful. I'm not sure when I might be called to leave on a mission, but I can take afternoon shifts until that time."

Their mother frowned. "I never knew I had such bossy children."

They laughed, and Kat hugged her. "You taught us

family sticks together during difficult times. We're only doing what you would expect and what we expect under the circumstances." She turned to Deirdre. "Are you going to call and ask Lloyd to help?"

"No, I'll ask him to stop by when he's got a day off. He may be able to get more information on Dad's condition than they'll tell us. When I checked in with him earlier, he said he was doing rounds, and keeping an eye on his patient that has stabilized. He'll be here as soon as possible."

"Sis, will you send us a list showing when we're to be here?" Gavin asked Deirdre.

"Yes. I'm taking Mom home, and I'll type up the list and send a copy to each of you. Then you write in the times you're certain you can be here."

"Sounds good. I've got to go to the fire station and explain what's going on to my Captain."

"I'll take the first shift from now until midnight," Cory said. "I want to help as much as possible before I get sent off, which might not happen soon or might be in a few hours."

"We understand." Scott put his hand on their younger brother's shoulder. "The rest of us need to go to work until our shifts are over. I'll relieve Cory, unless he gets called out before five."

"Cory, if you do, call me. I'll come to the hospital. I have the rest of the day off," Deirdre said. She turned to their Mom. "Let's go home, and you can rest."

"Not until I've seen your Dad."

"Of course. We'll go by the Intensive Care Unit on our way out."

* * *

Mrs. Cafferty put her fingers to her mouth when she saw her husband. Deirdre put an arm around her.

"The bruises will go away, Mom. It's the other problems he has to fight." Deirdre watched as her mother walked to the side of the bed and leaned down close to her father's head.

"Brody Cafferty, we've been together since we met in high school, and this is much too early for us to be parted. You fight for your life, for us, for all the future we can have yet. And," she added, leaning down close to his ear, "We're still going to get that motor home and travel the country. Don't let me down now." Her voice quivered as she spoke. When she tried to let go of him, his hand tightened on hers.

"I knew you were listening, and I love you more than the sun and the moon. Get well." She choked on the last words and kissed his hand. Trembling, she turned to her daughter. "He squeezed my hand. He'll get well."

The determination in her voice had Deirdre straightening her shoulders. When they started to leave, Deirdre turned back. "Dad, one of us will be in the waiting room until you wake up and get better. We're always near and praying for you." She swallowed through a tight throat as tears ran down her face.

Outside the ICU, Deirdre took out a tissue and wiped her face. Her Mom had her cloth handkerchief always nearby. "Let's go home, Mom. You need to rest."

* * *

Madison stopped by the office to speak with Captain Buchanan.

"Cory asked to leave, he said it was an emergency. He left so quick I didn't get to ask what the emergency was, but I expect it might be some type of accident to a family member. Do you know what happened?" the Captain asked.

"Cory just called me. His Dad's car was hit, and he was badly injured. All the family went to the hospital. Cory's taking the first shift to stay there in case his father's condition changes."

"I'm sure his family is upset. They're very close."

"Yes, they are. Mr. Cafferty came through surgery but is in critical condition in the ICU. I'm going to the hospital now, if that's all right with you."

"Certainly, call me and let me know how they're all doing."

"Will do, Captain."

Madison rushed to his car and drove to the hospital where Kat's Dad had been taken. When he arrived, he went up to the third floor, where he found Cory and Kat in the waiting room.

"Hi, Madison. Kat's just relieving me. It's kind of you to come by."

"How's your Dad?"

"Actually, the nurse said his vitals have been better since Mom visited. I called Mom, and she's insisting on coming back for a little while to see him. I've got to go, but Kat's on duty now. You two can visit." He winked and waved as he rushed to the elevator.

Madison sat down on the sofa by Kat. "How are you doing?"

"It's hard. Our parents have always been healthy. We used to worry about Dad being a cop, but he never got more than a few bruises on the job. It's ironic he got seriously hurt only now that he's retired."

"How did the accident happen?"

"From what we've been told, which isn't much, a new Mom glanced back at her baby and thought he was choking. In that instant, she ran a stop sign and T-boned Dad's car. Thankfully, the baby wasn't hurt, but the mother has a concussion, broken ribs, and a broken leg. Deirdre stopped to see her on her way out of the hospital."

"I imagine she feels awful."

"She does. Deirdre tried to tell her we weren't mad at her. Things happen. New babies can take your mind off what you're doing, or so I've been told."

"I guess you haven't had much time to make a decision about your future."

"Actually, I have. I told my parents what happened to me. Doing so, I realized my desire to be a strong woman and know how to protect myself came from that incident. I'd never resolved it until talking with them.

"The Chief wants me to come back as a detective. He said I'm good, but I take too many risks."

"A smart and observant man."

"I knew you'd say something like that, and I guess I agree I've been a bit reckless at times."

"A bit?" Madison raised his eyebrows.

"Well, you are also in your job, I'd bet."

"We go in with a plan and, unless it becomes necessary, we stick to it."

She made a disgruntled sound. "I bet lots of times you have to regroup."

"Whatever. Promise me you'll do as you told your Chief."

"Why?"

Madison had been trying to resist her, but now he leaned forward and hugged and kissed her. He whispered in her ear, "You are important to me, more than I want you to be."

She pushed him away. "What do you mean?"

"We both have dangerous jobs. Yours, not so much if you'd do it correctly and not get reckless. With mine, there will always be a degree of danger. If we fall in love and you want to keep your job, I fear our children might become orphans at some point."

"And you'd expect your wife to retire and be a sweet homebody."

He heard the sarcasm in her voice. "Yeah, I guess I would prefer that to happen."

"You have the wrong woman. I'm not the homebody type, and I don't like to cook."

"We can order dinner from one of those many places online."

"Forget it. I'm a career woman. One day I plan to be the police chief."

"Very ambitious. I guess I'd better stop seeing you, because I don't intend to retire from the SEALs anytime soon." He stood and took a deep breath. "I'll keep in touch with Cody to see how your Dad is doing."

It took all his willpower to walk casually to the elevator. He wanted to grab Kat and kiss her until she changed her mind. But that wouldn't be fair, considering where they were and what had happened.

When he got on the empty elevator, he cursed all the way to the first floor.

CHAPTER 13

Kat watched him go.

I'll get over this feeling. I'm not ready to be serious about anyone, especially a SEAL. She told herself Madison could be gone more than he'd be at home. *Then why do I feel like crying as I watch him walk away from me? We're not that tight. I've had too much time off.*

She blinked to keep back the tears, and her throat tightened with emotion she preferred to deny. *Once I'm back at work and busy, I'll forget all about Madison.* Kat sat back and tried to read the book she had on her reader. But the letters blurred, and her heart hurt. *Damn it. I need to get back to my job and be busy. Then I'll do fine.*

The elevator doors opened. For a second, Kat's spirits rose as she wondered if Madison had come back. It was her mother. "Mom, what are you doing here? You visited earlier today."

"Yes, and your father responds to my touch. I intend to go in and see him now. My children will have to realize I don't take orders when it concerns your father." She stood straight, as if daring Kat to stop her.

"I agree, Mom. Let's ring the bell and see if we can visit him."

The nurse smiled when she came to the door. "Mrs. Cafferty, he's been more alert since you were here this morning. He hasn't opened his eyes, but he's been following simple commands."

"Oh, good. Of course my husband is waiting to see me before he opens his eyes."

The nurse and Kat smiled as they followed her mother to the cubicle where her father lay in bed.

She walked directly to her husband and took his hand. "Brody, it's time for you to wake up. I'm sure you are holding back because I said when you're well we are going to travel. Open your eyes right now, or I'll find another man to travel with me."

Kat gasped. She knew her mother didn't mean it, but she still had been surprised.

They all watched as his eyelids fluttered and then opened. He looked at his wife and his lips moved. Kat's Mom leaned close to his mouth. When she straightened, she smiled. "I knew you were in there somewhere, taking a long rest. You deserve it. Your body took a beating, but I'm not letting you go, not yet."

A slight smile curved his lips as he tried to speak again. Kat's Mom leaned down. He raised his head enough to kiss her cheek. She moved back as tears ran down her face. The nurse handed Mrs. Cafferty a tissue and pulled up a chair for her to sit on.

"I'm here, Dad," Kat said. "Your tomboy daughter.

You won't be surprised to know your other daughter, who is much more organized than me, has us all set up so someone is in the waiting room if you need something."

When she saw his lips move, Kat stepped to the side of the bed and leaned down. Her father whispered, "I'm going to be fine. Not time to leave my family."

"Then do whatever these people say, and we'll get you home sooner." Seeing he wanted to speak again, Kat moved down close to his lips.

"Tell the kids I love them. Home soon."

"I'll give them your message, except for the home soon part. You have some healing to do before that happens. Be good and work hard."

Kat moved away and turned her back as her chest hurt and tears flooded her face. *I think I may have made the biggest mistake of my life.*

"Mom, I need to make a phone call." She hurried out of the unit and took out her cellphone. She still had his number and the base number. Her cell rang as she started to call him.

"Sis, this is Cory. Sorry, I can't be there to help anymore. See you."

Sinking onto the nearest chair, she knew his team was on its way out. That would be the only reason Cody would be so terse. Bent over, she cried all the tears she'd held back since her Dad's accident.

Her mother rushed to her side when she came out and saw her. "What happened?"

"I think Cody is gone on a mission."

"We knew that might happen." Mrs. Cafferty sat

back and studied her. "Ah, I know. You sent Madison away. I was afraid you'd do exactly that, and now you regret your words."

Kat nodded, unable to speak.

"Don't worry. I did that to your Dad. He was getting impatient, and I told him I wasn't certain he was the one."

Kat wiped her eyes and looked at her Mom. "You didn't."

"I did. In my youth, I was quite lovely."

"You still are, Mom."

"Thank you, sweetheart, but to finish my story, he went away. He told me to call if I changed my mind, but he might not still be available."

"Wow!"

"I knew he was the one, but I hadn't wanted to make it too easy for him. Still, when he said those words, he wasn't kidding. It took me about three days to get up my courage to call."

"What happened?"

"You know the rest. We dated and within six months decided to marry. A decision neither of us has ever regretted."

"Then you think I can handle a husband and my job."

"My goodness, did you really tell him the job was more important to you?"

"Pretty much."

"I think you might have to do a lot of sweet-talking, like I did to make things right with your father. If you think you love Madison, that is."

"I do. I know it's too soon after our divorces, but I never felt about my ex the way I do about him."

"Then go for it."

Kat hugged her Mom. "I love you and Dad so much."

"I know." She patted Kat's back. "Now, I'm tired. Your Dad told me to go rest, so I will."

"I can drive you and come back. Then one of us will bring your car home later."

"No, stay here. I'm fine. It's not that far."

She watched as her mother got on the elevator. *I hope things can work for Madison and me as well as they have for Mom and Dad.*

Feeling better about her future, she opened her tablet and began to read.

* * *

Madison listened as the Captain went over the mission. "We're going in quickly and hope to get rid of the rest of this specific group. Since our last visit to the Middle East, they've gotten more dangerous and have killed many innocent people. They want to take over an area that's essential for us to keep free.

"The locals help us, bring us info, and we're determined to keep them as friends, which means taking down this group. Any questions about the mission?"

"No," they all said, and then wandered off to find a place to rest until arrival.

After that, Madison knew they'd be working nonstop. He wished he'd had time to call Kat, but this break was probably better. She meant what she said. *I'll forget her. When other break-ups happened, it hasn't been difficult for me to move on. But then, I didn't care as much.*

Cory sat beside him. "I gather you're like me and having trouble getting to sleep."

"I know you must be worried about your Dad."

"Yes, but I'm trying to put it out of my mind. There's nothing I can do before I get back but work hard on our assignment, so we go home sooner."

"Why didn't you beg off this one? I thought you were going to another team?"

"There's a lot of meetings going on between the team leader and the higher-ups. Or so I've heard from some of the team members. They aren't expected to go out until those are completed. I asked to go with your team before Dad got hurt."

"Why?"

"I want more experience, and this is a good team. You all will set me straight if I mess up." He grinned, then grew serious. "I guess Kat's on your mind."

"I'd like to say no, but she is, and she told me to go away for good just before this assignment."

"Like I told you before, she's going to be hard to get."

"I'm not up to playing games. I'm through. If Kat wants to see me, it's up to her. Now go try to sleep. I'm going to. We'll regret it later if we don't get some rest."

Madison slept little. Even so, it seemed only a few hours before they were landing. *When we get inside the compound, I'll splash my face with cold water and shake off this sluggish feeling.*

The Captain stopped them from going directly to the barracks. "We have to move out now. The group we're after just hit another village and killed everyone. We're leaving in thirty minutes."

In the barracks, they all threw their personal items in lockers. Madison splashed cold water on his face, then made sure he had enough medical supplies in his pack.

"Everyone ready to go?" Bear asked.

"Yeah," they all hollered back.

"Then move out. We don't want the plane to leave without us."

The plane was two helos, and the group divided and hurried on. They flew over the dense forest. They weren't as lucky as last time. There was a full moon, so the helicopters let them off further from the target area.

Once they'd all touched ground and the helos took off, Bear motioned for them to gather around. He pulled out a map.

"Heath, you take your usual group and head north. I'll take mine to the south. Kijika will go straight and relay back to us what he sees. We'll attack at my command."

They all nodded and formed their groups. At Bear's signal, they headed out. Kijika waited until it was all quiet, and then slipped into the forest. He made no noise with the moccasins he wore, and the training he learned from his father and uncle, who still lived on the Reservation in Arizona.

With his darkened face and dark clothes, it was easy to move from tree to tree. He moved faster than the teams, and when he heard voices, he sank to the ground and crawled forward.

Many of the enemies sat around the fire. A few stood nearby. A man was tied to a pole, wood piled around his feet. A man, obviously the leader, circled him.

"Unless you tell us all you know, we will burn you alive."

So, the report was incorrect, the group didn't kill everyone in the village. "Bear, one prisoner, being threatened with being burned to death," Kijika whispered into his mouthpiece.

"We're getting close. Stay where you are. We'll be with you soon."

"What if they set fire to him?"

"Wait for us."

For once, Kijika wasn't sure he'd obey that order. He surveyed the group. About twenty stood around and another ten sat by the fire.

"I see about thirty," he whispered to Bear.

"Circle to the back of the camp, gather weeds and brush behind as many of the tents as you can. At my signal, start the fires."

"Will do."

It was easy to move behind the tents. All their interest was on the captive. Kijika knew how to quickly set small piles of brush up against the tent walls. He moved fast, and after finishing one side, slipped around the back of the area and moved to the remaining tents. He paused to see if anyone had spotted him.

Obviously not. Kijika continued his task. Then he heard Bear's order: "Set them on fire."

Running, he lit the first group of tents. The hostiles

quickly noticed the smoke. He got to the other side and lit the second group of tents. Moving swiftly, Kijika vanished into the dense woods and watched the confusion build in the enemy camp.

Bear and Heath's groups attacked with gunfire and grenades. By the time they were done, only a few of the enemy survived. Heath's group rounded them up and cuffed them. Kijika untied the captive.

"Thank you, thank you, but please, a woman was inside the last tent." He nodded to the left. "I saw her run into the woods."

"We'll find her," Bear said. "Kijika and Ranger, go look for her."

Kijika and Ranger set off in the direction the man indicated. Kijika easily picked up her footsteps and followed her trail.

"Wish we'd asked her name," Ranger said.

"No problem. We'll find the woman."

"Kijika, you are always so certain. But then, you've never been wrong."

Kijika held up a hand and stopped moving. "Shhh. I hear something. Do you hear the sound to the left?"

"Yes, but I also hear something rustling in front of us."

"Someone followed her. Let's separate. I'll follow her, and you go after whoever's trying to recapture her."

"Will do." Ranger turned toward the left and slipped out of sight.

Kijika smiled. He'd taught Ranger well. He'd wanted Kijika to give him lessons, and now those lessons would pay off.

The stumbling woman continued to make noise, and Kijika soon caught up with her. Frightened by Kijika's darkened face, she tried to fight him.

"Stop, I'm not the enemy. We were sent to rescue any hostages."

She looked up at his face. "How can I believe you?"

"I guess you'll have to take a chance. Once we return to the camp, you'll see that my friends have taken over."

"Did you kill the man they were pretending to torment?"

"Pretending?"

"Yes. I heard them say they knew someone was coming, but were not sure when you'd arrive."

Kijika immediately turned on his mic. "Bear, don't trust the prisoner."

He waited for a response. None. "Damn." To the woman, he said, "Come on, we have to walk fast."

"I'm not going anywhere. I'll find a place to hide and wait for your return. Go. Your men need you."

"I'll come back and get you." He ran toward the camp and radioed Ranger to meet him there. "The team might be in trouble."

* * *

Ranger ran back toward camp. When he got closer, he ducked down and crawled. The man they'd freed stood beside the fire. He appeared relaxed and friendly as he spoke to several of the SEALs. Ranger made a bird sound as Kijika had taught him, and he saw Bear's head go up. Then Ranger chirped rapidly, the sound a signal of danger.

Bear barked to his men, "Make certain all the guns are emptied and broken. Put this guy," he gestured at the former hostage, "in the middle tent with a guard on the front and back."

"What? I'm a victim. Why do I have to be guarded? Give me a gun. I'll help you."

"We may have our hands full. We don't have time to worry about you. Heath, come here." Bear whispered in Heath's ear, "Kijika or Ranger signaled danger. The only danger can be that guy." He nodded toward the man they'd rescued. "Watch him. If he tries anything, shoot him."

"Yes, Sir."

"Take Gordy. Have him guard the back of the tent."

"Will do. But that only leaves you, Cody, Professor and Hawke out here."

"Kijika and Ranger are nearby. Since we have all the captives tied up, that only leaves the prisoner as the possible danger."

"It all sounds complicated to me."

"I know you can never trust these guys. They are clever, I'll give them that."

"And he did tell us about the woman who left us with two fewer men here."

"I hope the woman isn't in on this, or we've been shafted."

"We'll go with the information we have and be on our toes."

Kijika messaged Bear, "Enemies behind us. Get

ready. Larger group. We'll stay here and hit from behind."

"Be careful," Bear radioed back. He motioned to Cory, Doc and Hawke to hide, leaving an empty, silent camp. They left the bodies on the ground around the fire pit.

Kijika watched as a large group of men silently slipped through the thick brush and around trees. A man in the front raised his hand and brought it down. They rushed the camp. As the last one passed Kijika, he and Ranger fired at their backs. Several men fell as the group continued toward the camp.

Once inside the camp, the leader put up his hand to halt the approach of his men. It was apparent by his expression he didn't understand what had happened. He said something to his men in their language. Madison, who Bear had kept by his side to translate, whispered, "He's confused, and told his men to spread out and look for survivors."

"We don't want them to do that," Bear said, and ordered in a loud voice, "Attack."

All of Bear's team came out of hiding, firing on the confused men. Ranger and Kijika ran forward to join the team. In a few minutes, the attackers were tied up or dead.

Madison ignored the bullet that caught him in his upper chest. His breathing wasn't affected, so he slid a thick pad of square bandages against the spot and taped it. Then he moved between the injured men. Enemies or not, they needed treatment. *Luckily, except for myself, our group looks good.*

Once they were satisfied all the enemies were unarmed, Cory came to see if he might help Madison. "What can I do?"

Madison handed him a bottle. "Pour it on any open wounds to help disinfect and clean the area. I'll be along to put on bandages."

Cory stared at the blood that had seeped through Madison's quickly applied bandage. Madison put his finger to his lips and said, "I'm good. Don't tell anyone. The helos will be here soon. I'll have it checked when we return to quarters."

Cory frowned, but did as he was told. When the helos arrived, they moved the wounded first.

Ranger and Kijika went back out to retrieve the woman. Kijika whistled and was surprised to hear a whistle back. He glanced to the left, went a few steps, and stood under a tree.

"You can come down now," he called up to her.

"I went too high. I'm a good climber, but I sometimes fall coming down. Move, so I won't hit you if I can't make it all the way out of this tree the right way."

Ranger laughed. "I'll come up and help. Kijika can stand by in case either of us falls."

Once she was on the ground, the woman, dirty and disheveled, smiled. "Thank you doesn't seem enough."

"You can always put a fortune into our secret Swiss accounts," Ranger said.

For a second, she looked stunned. Both men laughed.

"Ranger has a weird sense of humor," Kijika said. "There is no Swiss bank account."

She laughed and then frowned. “I thought I’d been misled, and you were the bad guys.”

“Forgive me,” Ranger said. “I’m stupid, and sometimes after a battle I make silly jokes. I didn’t realize I’d scare you.”

Suddenly, she straightened and kicked Ranger, knocking him down. “Smartass, I knew you were kidding. I’m a Secret Service agent, but what if I’d been a captive? It wouldn’t be funny at all. I ought to report you, but since you and your friend saved my ass, I’ll let it go.”

Both men looked surprised. She laughed. “Do you think a real captive would climb a tree and hang on?”

“Maybe.” Ranger straightened his shoulders. “One who’s brave and scared and pulls it together to survive. There are brave women without training.”

“I guess so. Let’s get to your camp. I want out of here and to have a nice, hot shower.”

“Don’t we all,” Ranger mumbled as they headed toward the camp.

CHAPTER 14

Once on the plane to return to the main base, Captain Buchanan walked among his men congratulating them for getting the whole crew, including the prisoner. He talked to each individually. When he got to Madison, he leaned closer.

Madison had tried to turn his wounded side away from the Captain, but his superior ordered, "Turn and face me. What the hell is that red on your clothes?" He reached out and ripped Madison's shirt open.

"When were you going to have that taken care of, here or in the States?"

"Here. I just didn't want you to worry."

"Damn, I'm *supposed* to worry and know everything that happens to my men."

"It's fine. I poured antiseptic over it and put on a bandage."

"Your tetanus shot better be up-to-date, or I'll personally kick your ass."

"Of course it is."

"Well, with you, apparently, there is 'no of course'. You take care of others and ignore yourself. I haven't forgotten the last time you tried to hide an injury while on a mission to the Middle East."

"That was nothing."

"No, just a sprained wrist that swelled significantly. You almost ruined your chance to stay on the team."

"We were being shot at and only had half our usual force. If I didn't help, we might have been killed or taken prisoner."

"If you do this again, I promise I'll maim you even worse. Where's Cory? He was with you."

Cory stepped forward. "Here, Captain."

"Why didn't you report this injury?"

"I was ordered to keep quiet."

"And you always obey orders?"

"Yes, Sir."

"Use your head and your instincts next time. There are situations where it will be necessary to speak with a higher-ranked officer."

"Yes, Sir. I won't forget, Captain."

"When we get back, you'll be cleaning all the guns before getting permission to leave the base." He frowned at Madison. "You will go to the base hospital, and once you're released, I have many jobs you can do before receiving any leave. Is that understood?"

"Yes, Captain."

Madison watched the Captain walk off.

"Sorry about getting you in trouble," he said to Cory. "Captain Buchanan will reconsider and let you off when we get home. Don't worry."

"I'm not. The Captain was right. Next time I'll report you," Cory gave him the finger and sat beside Madison.

"You mad at me?"

"Nope. I'm learning all the time."

"Still think I'd be good for your sister?"

"Not unless you start taking better care of yourself. I don't want Kat to be a widow."

"Yeah, I guess you're right. Anyway, Kat's through with me."

"Hah, you don't know Kathleen very well. She'll lead you on a merry chase before she says yes."

"Kathleen. I like the full name better than Kat."

"She only lets Mom and Dad occasionally call her Kathleen, and it's usually when they're mad at her."

"If I can convince Kat to marry me, she'll let me use her full name. Wait and see."

"This will be even more fun to watch than I thought."

Madison did feel dizzy, but he'd never admit it. He lay down when Cory left and closed his eyes. When he woke to put on his seat belt for landing, his skin felt hot. *Oh, yay, an infection has set in. I guess I gave myself that antibiotic shot too late.*

* * *

Cory made it home for Sunday dinner. No one asked questions, but admitted they were glad to see him.

"Yesterday, I mostly slept. I'm hungry now."

"You came to the right place. Mom made your favorite chicken and dumplings," Gavin said.

"Who's staying with Dad, and how's he doing?"

"Lloyd had a whole day off. He's staying until three, when I'll relieve him, and he'll come to Mom's to eat," Scott said. "Dad's doing much better and hopes to come home in a week or so. He'll need some rehab, but at least he'll be back in his own bed, as he puts it."

"I'm glad Lloyd has some time with Dad, and I'll be glad to see him. With my SEAL work and his medical residency, we don't see much of each other."

"That's what you get for going into different professions than the rest of us," Gavin said and gave him a big body hug. "Glad to see you back safe and sound."

Their Mom came out carrying a large bowl of chicken and dumplings. Kat followed with a platter of fresh green beans and mushrooms.

She saw Cory and raised her eyebrows. "You're back," she said as she placed the platter on the table.

"Yes, and I'm fine."

"Did all your team come back safe?"

"Are you asking about Maddy?"

"Only his family calls him by that name."

"I know."

Their mother called Kat to the kitchen door. "Put the rolls and butter on the table, please."

Kat had just placed the basket of rolls on the table when Cory added, "Everyone's fine except Madison, who's in the hospital."

"What?" She sat abruptly in the nearest chair.

"He'll be fine. He got his shoulder wounded while, helping others."

Kat felt the eyes of her family on her and couldn't

stop the blush that heated her cheeks. *Damn, now they'll know I care about him.*

Her Mom bent over her. "He's fine, and I'm certain he's in the military hospital, where they'll take good care of him."

Taking a deep breath, Kat sat up straight. "I agree. I," she shrugged her shoulders, "was only surprised he got hurt. You all can quit staring at me. My reaction means nothing. We decided to not see each other anymore."

"I bet that was your idea," Scott mumbled.

"Oh, quit being a know-it-all," she said and stuck out her tongue at him.

"That's enough, children." Their mother gave them the evil eye, as they used to call it, the one that always made them stop whatever they were doing.

"I'll visit Dad this afternoon when all of you have gone on your way. I want to see Lloyd. It's been a while."

Kat started passing the food around. She sat at the end of the table and was relieved when the conversation changed to football and who would win the Super bowl.

After lunch, Kat tagged Cory to help her with the dishes. He reluctantly agreed and followed her to the sink. "I'll dry. But why doesn't Mom use her dishwasher?"

"You know she's afraid it will hurt her fine china. Okay, I'll wash, and you can tell me about Madison's injuries and how long he expects to be in the hospital."

"Why are you interested? Madison said you broke up with him."

"I did. I'm back on the job and have no time for a man who's away from home more than I am."

"Sounds like you're trying to convince yourself. Are you afraid to love Madison because he's a SEAL?"

"Of course not. Still, if we ever had children, one of us would have to change jobs."

"Then don't have kids," Cory said bluntly. "I don't plan on having children, not with my job. Maybe I'll wait until I leave the SEALs, but then I'd probably not want them that late in life."

"Really? That's a shame."

"Why?"

She grinned. "Because I want to see a little Cory and his sister running around."

"What's good for you is good for me."

They were both quiet as they finished cleaning the kitchen. Kat put the apron she'd borrowed on a nearby chair. She cupped Cory's face in her hands.

"When you were born, I was five. I thought of you as my baby doll."

Cory blushed, and Kat laughed. "You loved the attention then, and I adored you."

"I never knew why I always seemed to have a special feeling for you."

"Now you know, and I demand you give me some little Cory's to spoil."

He shook his head. "Not unless you have some babies I can spoil." He pulled her into his arms. "I love you, Sis, and now I've made you cry. Go wipe your tears. I'll take you to see Maddy."

She sniffed. "Do you call Madison Maddy at work?"

"Hell, no. He'd beat me up."

In the bathroom, Kat looked at herself in the mirror

and thought about Madison. *You love him, be brave enough to admit it, and don't let the best man you know, besides Dad and the brothers, get away.*

She feared it might already be too late.

Cory knocked on the door. "Hurry up, I haven't got all day."

"Why not?" she asked when she came out of the bathroom.

"I'm meeting some of the guys and their wives at the beach for a picnic."

"They include a single guy like you?" she teased.

"We're all family. If you behave, I'll take you with me. It might be good for you to talk with some of the wives."

"Hmm, maybe. We'll see."

* * *

Cory found out Madison's room number, and they took the elevator up to the fourth floor. The nurses at the desk, directed them to Room 426.

Kat heard the nurses giggling as she and her brother walked off. "I think they're admiring your backside," she teased, and Cory's face turned bright red.

"Stop it," he growled.

"Ha-ha. You'll find a lady yet. Or she'll find you."

The door to Madison's room was shut. Cory knocked and cracked it open to look inside. The nurse was bandaging his shoulder.

"Come on in," he called out. "The nurse is almost finished."

The tall brunette smiled and motioned for Cory to

enter. "Keep him company. He's getting restless and wants to leave us too soon."

"I have someone else with me," Cory said. "Is it all right for him to have more visitors?"

"As long as he keeps his arm still, so the intravenous drip doesn't get stopped up from his movements."

"Maybe she'd better stay outside," Cory said and smiled. Then he opened the door all the way, and Kat stepped inside.

"If you'd rather I leave, I will," she said and took a small step toward his bed.

The nurse smiled and slipped by her.

"I thought you were through with me and all men."

"Women have the right to be wrong occasionally."

"Occasionally?" Madison quirked an eyebrow up and didn't smile.

"And stupid once in a while." Kat's lips curved up as her heart pounded in her chest. Was she too late to make amends?

"Come here." He held out his hand.

Cory left the room, but neither of them noticed as they stared at each other.

"Did you just come to tell me you hope I get well soon?"

"Partially."

"And what's the other part?"

"A lot has happened since you've been gone. I think you know Dad's still in the hospital."

"Yes. How's he doing?"

"Much better. Hopefully, he'll come home next Friday and get rehab for a while. Once he's completely well, he's promised Mom they'll get a motor home and travel. We'll all miss them, but it will be good for them and make Mom very happy."

"Good. Now, what's the other reason you're here?"

"Watching Mom and Dad come through his accident together was an eye-opener for me. I remember when Dad was first on the police force, he was out on the streets working rotating shifts. Mom got quiet at times. I realize now she was worried for his safety."

"Your Dad did well and became the Police Chief, from what you've told me."

"He did." Kat smiled at a memory. "He took me with him to see his new office. It impressed me. I told him I'd be Chief one day. I wanted to work in that big room. He chuckled and said it came with a lot of responsibility. I shrugged and said I could do it." She laughed. "I had no idea what I was talking about, but he didn't discourage me."

"Your parents are so much like mine. They were worried about my desire to go into SEAL training, but they didn't try and talk me out of it. If I'm ever a parent, I'd like to be as good a one as our parents."

"That's what I wanted to talk with you about. I never gave much thought about being a mother. I've been driven all my life by my determination to be as strong and good a cop as any of the men."

"I know."

His cellphone rang. Kat took it from the bedside table and put it in his hand.

He looked at the display, and answered, "Hi, Mom. No, really, I'm fine. They're going to let me out of here in a few days. Once the infection is gone. I'll still be on pills for a while, instead of the intravenous line. Yes, they're sure it will heal completely."

Kat's nerves got the best of her. She stood and went to the door. Madison waved for her to come back, but she only smiled and kept going.

It wasn't the right time to tell him, not yet. I'll wait until he's released and well. That will be soon enough. Coward. The word echoed in her head.

* * *

Kat was surprised to see Cory seated in the main waiting room. "Didn't you get bored?"

"A little, but I want to take you to the beach with me. You need to talk to the wives. Did you say everything you wanted to Madison?"

"No. His parents called, and I slipped out of the room. I guess I'm not quite ready to have a serious discussion with him. When he's well, I'll have him over for dinner."

Cory frowned. "I thought you were braver than that, Kat."

"Wait until you find someone you really like. Then I'll remind you of this conversation."

"That's a long, long time off."

"Maybe. Let's go. I'm looking forward to meeting these ladies."

"Okay. Do you want to change clothes?"

"Stop at my place. It'll only take me a moment to put on shorts and a cooler top. How about you?"

"I'll come up and change. I have my bathing suit and a towel with me."

* * *

The wives were not at all what Kat had expected. Some had interesting jobs, and others loved being at home with their children, even ones who'd had busy careers before they married.

"I just went back to work," Emma said. "I had an opportunity to teach at the school where Melissa attends, and I couldn't pass up the opportunity.

"Don't get me wrong, I love my children, but I did miss teaching. My parents have moved to San Diego for part of the year. They wanted to see more of their grandchildren and get away from the cold and snow. I've been lucky. They agreed to keep our younger ones for me during the school year. My parents go home during the summer. It worked out well for all of us."

The other wives joined in and explained how they'd all found what worked for their family.

"Do you still want to be a detective?" one of the wives asked.

"Maybe, for a while. But if I had children, I think I'd want to be like my Mom. Stay at home and be there when needed. She gave up a teaching career after my older sister and brother were born. There are six of us. Cory is my youngest brother."

"Wow. How was it growing up in such a large family?" Kayla asked.

"Fun, crazy, wonderful and terrible," Kat said and

grinned. "My sister and I are the only girls."

Cheryl leaned forward. "It sounds like a lot of fun for you and your siblings. How are your parents doing?"

"They've survived rather well." Kat explained about her Dad's accident. "But he'll be home soon, and Mom finally convinced him to travel part of the year. I'm certain they'll enjoy it, but my siblings and I are going to have a difficult time getting used to not having them nearby. It'll be a new experience."

Finally, they moved on other subjects, and Kat was fascinated by their conversations. When they all got up to leave, they hugged her.

"We're going to lunch next Saturday. Why not join us?" Kayla suggested. She told Kat the name of the restaurant.

"I'd love to, if I'm not on duty."

Kayla gave her a phone number. "I'm home most of the time. You can let me know."

"Great." Kat joined her brother, who'd been exercising on the beach with the other men.

"Did you have a good time?" he asked.

"I did, and it was certainly insightful."

"Good now go back to the hospital and put Madison's mind at rest. Tell him how you feel."

"I have to change. Drop me off at home, and I'll drive myself over later."

"Are you going to change your mind?"

"No. I know what I want. It took me some time to figure out what that is, but seeing Mom and Dad helped clarify it."

"Okay. I'm heading home after I let you out."

CHAPTER 15

Kat waved goodbye and watched as Cory drove out of sight. She let herself into her condo and smiled when she glanced at the new lock. *From the first, he's wanted to take care of me. I know Madison is different from any other man I've met and dated. He's not at all like my ex-husband. But have we known each other long enough?*

She threw off her clothes and got in the shower. As Kat rinsed the sand off, she thought about what to say to him, and how. By the time she dressed and got in the car, she almost shook from nerves. *What if he tells me he's not interested anymore?*

The drive seemed short, and she sat in the military hospital's parking lot a minute to take some deep breaths and calm herself. *I think I'd be less nervous in a gunfight.* The thought made her smile, but once on the elevator, the nerves came back.

The nurse, who'd worked on Madison's bandages earlier, was waiting to get on the elevator when the doors opened on the fourth floor. She smiled at Kat.

"I think he's been hoping you'd come back. Every time one of us goes into the room, his smile fades."

"Thanks for telling me. I need the encouragement."

When the nurse got on the elevator, she held the door and said, "Your man's a great catch. If you don't take him, one of us might." She was still grinning when the elevator's door closed.

Kat took a deep breath and slowly walked to Madison's door. Her throat was dry, and she coughed. Realizing it was now or never, she pushed the door open.

Madison lay on his side, eyes closed. Kat heard a soft snore. Relief flowed through her. She had a reprieve, time to settle herself. Kat moved the small chair closer to his bed and sat to study him. He had a strong face, one she trusted.

She thought about her marriage. She'd been caught up in her ex-husband's good looks and flattery. Madison wasn't as handsome and slick as her ex-husband, but he had the face of a man you could rely on, someone who didn't let people down. Too her, he was the most handsome man she'd ever dated.

How had his wife ever let him get away? He said she liked to party and he didn't, and she got restless staying at home when he wanted to relax. In those ways, she and Madison were much alike.

His eyelids began to flicker, and he opened his eyes. "How long have you been sitting here?" he asked in a sleepy voice.

She shrugged. "I don't know. Watching you sleep peacefully is comforting."

"In what way?"

"Even in your sleep, I see your strength, your goodness."

"Wow, what a compliment."

"I went to the beach today and talked with the other SEALs' wives."

"What did they say?"

"Lots of things. They talked about their husbands and children, and how life changed for them when they married into the SEALs' type of lifestyle."

"And what did you think?"

"I realized how happy they were and how each had found their own place in the family and in the outside world."

She stopped talking and looked at the full moon outside his window.

"I'm going to get well and return to my SEAL team."

"I know, and I'm glad."

He took her hand. "I wish I could promise I'd give it all up for you. But I can't. It's too much a part of me, of who I am, and I can't leave my team."

"I wouldn't have understood before meeting the wives and some of your team members. The families are all one big team."

"You do understand now?"

"Yes, and that each wife has found her own way of taking care of the family, being all right when the husbands have to leave and finding something of worth in their individual lives."

"Wow, you did learn a lot this afternoon."

"I did, but I'd already made up my mind before I met the wives. Meeting them didn't change it."

Kat looked down at their hands, fingers intertwined. She hadn't even noticed when she took hold of him.

"I fully understand you have your career and want to be the future Police Chief. I admire you for your determination."

"You're wrong."

"About what?"

"There's something I want to be more than Chief."

"Really? Are you going to run for elected office?"

She laughed. "No, silly. As soon as you're able, I intend to marry you, whether you want me or not," she added with a smile. Madison's face looked pale and shocked. "But if you've changed your mind …"

He pulled her partway across him and kissed her, hard. "Shut up. Of course I want you." He winced and had to let her go. "Don't move too far away. Hold my hand."

Kat did as he said and waited for him to speak.

"Are you absolutely certain of your decision?"

"Yes."

"Good, because as soon as they release me, we're going to get rings and get married."

"No big wedding?" she asked and pretended to look sad.

"If you really can't do without it, I'll put up with all the mess to get you."

She grinned. "I had all that the first time. It didn't end well. What do you say about asking for a few days off, and we elope to Las Vegas? I've never been there."

"Are you for real? I had the same idea, but I thought you'd hit me if I suggested it. There is one other idea

I've thought about for our honeymoon. We might rent a cabin up in the mountains and do nothing but make love and occasionally eat to keep up our strength."

Kat put her hands out like she was weighing the options. "Vegas with lots of people or a quiet cabin all alone. Can you put up with just me for a few days?"

"A few days? Honey, we're going for a week, and then we'll go visit my parents for a few days. I have enough leave available. I didn't take much time off the past two years except when Dad got sick."

"Then just tell your Captain where we will be, and I'll tell my parents. We'll go to the courthouse with them as witnesses and get married."

"Sounds great." He ran his finger along the side of her face. "I tried to tell myself it didn't hurt when you sent me away, but it did. We must ask Cory to be a witness, too. He never lost faith in our happy ending."

"I told him he has to get married and give me more nieces and nephews. He challenged me to do the same for him."

"He's young. Give him time to become a worn-out old SEAL, then he'll come around."

"Ah, so that's how I got you."

"I didn't mean it quite that way."

"You are not a worn-out old SEAL. You are in the prime of life. I got you just in time."

He pulled her close and kissed her. "I'll see you never regret this decision."

"And I'll do the same for you."

"There is one place we need to go first tomorrow when they let me out of here. All the couples have gotten their rings at the same place. A small jewelry shop with a funny old man. You won't want to believe him, but he's pretty smart."

"I can't wait. I'm going to sleep right here tonight and make sure the doctor discharges you tomorrow."

* * *

Once Madison was released, they headed to the jewelry shop after getting directions from Captain Buchanan. He'd told his friend and commanding officer the good news, but to keep it to himself, and Madison got the time off for his wedding and honeymoon.

The bell rang as they walked into the shop. An old man came through the curtains at one side of the shop and smiled.

"You are the last one in your group. I thought I might not be here to meet you. And this is your lovely lady. A brave lady. I have read about you in the paper, Detective Cafferty."

Kat smiled. "And I've heard about you. You seem to know a lot about his group, she nodded toward Madison, and yet only good things have happened since they've gotten their rings at your shop."

"True, but there will be hard times. Everyone has them. Only remember those are the tested times that make us stronger.

"I have a special set of rings for your fiancé and you." The mysterious old man retrieved a box from under the counter and opened it. "When presented as a gift, as you both will be doing in exchanging rings at the ceremony, it is said the rings have healing properties and bring the wearer magical powers of protection. They can also instill power and influence. These are bright, lime-green peridots."

"They're beautiful, especially with the diamonds surrounding the main stone," Kat said. "I like the plain, slim wedding band. It doesn't take away from the dazzling engagement ring, and will be more appropriate for me to wear at work. But it must be expensive."

"Don't worry. It is not more than you can afford," the jeweler reassured her.

Still looking doubtful, she turned to Madison. "What do you think?"

"I think it's almost as gorgeous as your bright green eyes."

"For you, Sir," the jeweler said. "This gold band has two smaller peridot stones and with a small diamond on either side.

"Much like those my teammates wear. How much is all of this?"

As he'd had heard from his teammates, the price was lower than it should be, but the jeweler explained about returning the rings many years from now.

"The others explained that to me," Madison said.

The old man smiled in satisfaction. "Then I'll wrap these up for you."

Madison paid for the rings. They were almost out the door when the jeweler called after them, "You will have many children and long lives."

Kat turned with a frown. "No more than three."

The jeweler only smiled and waved.

When they got in the car, Kat said, "He's put a charm or something on us."

Madison laughed.

"I'll have my own bedroom after three children," she warned him and moved closer to the window.

He pulled her back against him. "Do you think you'll be able to resist me?"

"I'll try," but her words came out weakly. "Maybe we'll be tired of each other by that time."

Madison put the car in Drive and pulled away from the curb, saying smugly, "It'll never happen."

* * *

At the courthouse, marriage certificate in hand, they headed to the judge's office. Madison stopped in front of the door and looked at Kat.

"Are you certain you won't regret having only your parents and Cory here with us? Mom and Dad weren't able to come, but we'll be visiting them."

"They can be our witnesses. We'll surprise the rest after the fact."

The judge stood as they opened the door. "Come with me. I always dislike having a wedding in my office. It doesn't seem right." He led them down the hall and into what he called a conference room. When he walked in, they stopped in the doorway and stared in shock. Captain Buchanan and his wife, Madison's teammates, their wives and Kat's family filled the room.

They all yelled, "Surprise!"

"Mom, you told all these people?"

"Yes. And Cody told your team, Madison."

Captain Buchanan laughed. "You didn't think we'd miss this, did you? The last holdout of our team to be married."

"I've been married before."

"Yes, but you were able to keep that one secret and it didn't work. You have to have our blessings, and this one will be happy and prosperous," the Captain said, and everyone nodded in agreement.

Kat looked down at her only fancy dress, one her mother had given her when told of their upcoming marriage. The white dress matched her personality, elegant without frills.

"You look beautiful," her Mom said.

"You do," Madison added.

"Let's get this wedding started," the judge said, but he was smiling.

All Kat remembered later were the vows and the love that shone in her new husband's face. He whispered, "I will love and cherish you forever and beyond."

When tears came into her eyes, he kissed them away.

"All right," Scott said. "Let's head home. Mom has a wedding feast ready, and I want a piece of that beautiful wedding cake."

When they got in the car, Kat sat tight against him. "I ought to have known no one in my family would ever have a quiet, small wedding."

"I hope you liked it. I loved it."

She looked at him. "Why?"

"Now I feel like I'm really part of the family."

"I'm glad. If you ever try to leave me, I'll have my brothers hogtie you and bring you back."

"As long as I can move, I'll find my way home to you."

"All right, enough sweet talk. I'm getting hungry."

Madison chuckled and started the car. "And that's the practical side of my wife."

EPILOGUE

One Year Later

Madison held her hand and wiped her brow as another pain hit her. "I swear we will not have a herd of kids," she said from between gritted teeth.

"Your mother said it gets easier each time."

"Do you want me to hit you?"

"Do it if it will make you happy."

"You are too agreeable. Look at you, all relaxed and smiling. Don't smile."

Madison bit his lip, trying to obey his wife.

"Send Mom in. You are too handsome and not worried enough."

He laughed. "I'm too handsome? No one's ever told me that before."

"Get out and send in my mother, who'll be much more understanding."

"I'm going." He kissed her brow and then her lips. His hand rubbed across her belly, and then he kissed the area where the baby moved. "Love you both. Hurry up and get born, little squirt. Mom's getting angry at us both."

"I am not angry at our son, just his father. Get Mom."

"Yes, Princess. I do as you command."

He saw her struggle not to laugh as he left the room.

When he reached the waiting room, which was full of Caffertys and his parents, his mother-in-law patted his back sympathetically.

"She wants you," he told her. "My wife is angry with me right now."

Gavin said, "They all get that way." Scott nodded.

"I think I'll be very old before I consider marriage," Cody said.

"I agree." Lloyd looked at Gavin and Scott. "You two were very brave."

"Hah," Deirdre's husband said. "I remember we all paced the floor and sweated when our wives had our children. Madison's not as bad as a few of us."

"Good to hear, but Mom Cafferty, if you don't get in there, she may come and get you, swearing all the way."

Mrs. Cafferty shook her head. "She learned all those swear words from her brothers and her buddies on the police force."

Ten minutes later, they got the word for Madison to come to his wife's room. "She's ready to deliver, and I know both of you wanted Daddy present," the nurse said.

He ran to the birthing room and took hold of Kat's hand.

"Soon," she said, "we'll hold our son's hand. I'm excited."

"Not scared?"

"I don't think so. Mom had six and survived."

Madison started to make a remark and decided it might not be the best time.

Their seven-pound, three-ounce boy slipped out quickly. The nurses handed the newborn to Madison. For a second, the baby opened his eyes and blinked.

"I think he may have your beautiful green eyes, Kat."

"Eye color can change," a nurse said.

Kat took their baby into her arms. This time he opened his eyes longer.

"They're dark green. Mom said mine were the same way. I'm the only green-eyed person in our immediate family." She smiled at Madison. "You must have a little Irish in you, and our ancestors are blessing us."

* * *

A month later, Kat smiled at her husband as he held their son. "You handle him like an old pro. I'm sure that's the only reason our mothers left after the first week, seeing how good you were doing."

"I got a book on babies about what they needed, and how to handle them."

"I never saw you read it."

"I hid it when you were around. I knew you'd tease me, and then you'd tell the team, and I'd never have lived it down. They already like to call me Professor because I read so much."

"I'll never tell. It is nice to have a husband who knows what to do. I need to read your book."

"No, you're a natural, beautiful Mom. Look at how Cody Madison Carney looks at you. He adores you already. Here, you hold him for a while."

Kat smiled at her son and added, "Yeah, he'll adore me until he reaches his teens."

"Between you and me, our children won't have a chance to misbehave."

"Remember, my father was the chief of police, and we didn't fear him. They'll misbehave, but I think our children will be surprised at how many tricks we know to catch them."

"You're talking in the plural. Are you satisfied with having a big family?"

"Three is big."

"Four is bigger, two boys and two girls."

"You are ordering the sexes of our children?"

"I shouldn't have put that out in the universe."

"No, because now we'll probably have all the rest girls."

Madison leaned over and kissed her and their son. "I love you and him and any others we have. You have changed my life for the better in so many ways. Why are you crying?"

"Because I love you and him so much. I've become a watering pot."

"Don't worry, the book said that will pass, and you'll be back to your ornery self."

"If I had hold of that book now, I'd throw it at you."

Laughing, they held each other and their son close. Sunlight shone brightly in the room and covered them in a warm glow.

The End

ALSO BY RACHEL MCNEELY

Special Forces: Operation Alpha:

The SEAL's Surprise Baby

The SEAL's Surprise Bride

The SEAL's Surprise Twin

The SEAL's Surprise Mission

The SEAL's Surprise Marriage

The SEAL's Surprise Mate

The SEAL's Surprise Rescue

Others:

His Intriguing Imposter

The Persistent Suitor

The Rouge Suitor

The Warrior Suitor

The American Suitor

The Noble Suitor

The Earl's Undaunted Bride

The Duke's Unexpected Bride

The Duke's Blind Temptation

Sandstones Ghostly Secrets

Bewitching the Marquis

ABOUT THE AUTHOR

Born in Florida, Rachel McNeely's early dreams included being a movie star. Of course, it didn't happen. Later, she escaped into daydreams full of fascinating stories. Her friends had to endure her reading those tales to them when she began to put them to paper.

There were detours in her life for marriage, children, and going back to college. But, she continued to be an avid reader and dream of the day she'd have a book published. Once her children were grown and she had time to write, she joined a writer's group and her dreams of writing and publishing came true.

facebook.com/RachelMcNeelyAuthor
amazon.com/Rachel-McNeely
bookbub.com/authors/rachel-mcneely

There are many more books in this fan fiction world than listed here, for an up-to-date list go to www.AcesPress.com

You can also visit our Amazon page at: http://www.amazon.com/author/operationalpha

Special Forces: Operation Alpha World

Christie Adams: Charity's Heart
Denise Agnew: Dangerous to Hold
Shauna Allen: Awakening Aubrey
Brynne Asher: Blackburn
Linzi Baxter: Unlocking Dreams
Jennifer Becker: Hiding Catherine
Alice Bello: Shadowing Milly
Heather Blair: Rescue Me
Anna Blakely: Rescuing Gracelynn
Amy Briggs: Saving Sarah
Julia Bright: Saving Lorelei
Victoria Bright: Surviving Savage
Cara Carnes: Protecting Mari
Kendra Mei Chailyn: Beast
Melissa Kay Clarke: Rescuing Annabeth
Samantha A. Cole: Handling Haven
Sue Coletta: Hacked
Melissa Combs: Gallant
Anne Conley: Redemption for Misty
KaLyn Cooper: Rescuing Melina
Liz Crowe: Marking Mariah
Sarah Curtis: Securing the Odds
Jordan Dane: Redemption for Avery

Tarina Deaton: Found in the Lost
KL Donn: Unraveling Love
Riley Edwards: Protecting Olivia
PJ Fiala: Defending Sophie
Nicole Flockton: Protecting Maria
Michele Gwynn: Rescuing Emma
Casey Hagen: Shielding Nebraska
EM Hayes: Gambling for Ashleigh
Desiree Holt: Protecting Maddie
Kathy Ivan: Saving Sarah
Jesse Jacobson: Protecting Honor
Silver James: Rescue Moon
Becca Jameson: Saving Sofia
Kate Kinsley: Protecting Ava
Heather Long: Securing Arizona
Gennita Low: No Protection
Kirsten Lynn: Joining Forces for Jesse
Margaret Madigan: Bang for the Buck
Kimberly McGath: The Predecessor
Rachel McNeely: The SEAL's Surprise Baby
KD Michaels: Saving Laura
Wren Michaels: The Fox & The Hound
Kat Mizera: Protecting Bobbi
Mary B Moore: Force Protection
LeTeisha Newton: Protecting Butterfly
Angela Nicole: Protecting the Donna
MJ Nightingale: Protecting Beauty
Sarah O'Rourke: Saving Liberty
Victoria Paige: Reclaiming Izabel
Anne L. Parks: Mason
Debra Parmley: Protecting Pippa

Lainey Reese: Protecting New York
TL Reeve and Michele Ryan: Extracting Mateo
Elena M. Reyes: Keeping Ava
Angela Rush: Charlotte
Rose Smith: Saving Satin
Jenika Snow: Protecting Lily
Lynn St. James: SEAL's Spitfire
Dee Stewart: Conner
Harley Stone: Rescuing Mercy
Jen Talty: Burning Desire
Megan Vernon: Protecting Us

Police and Fire: Operation Alpha World

Freya Barker: Burning for Autumn
KaLyn Cooper: Justice for Gwen
Aspen Drake: Sheltering Emma
Deanndra Hall: Shelter for Sharla
Barb Han: Kace
CM Steele: Guarding Hope
Reina Torres: Justice for Sloane
Stacey Wilk: Stage Fright

As you know, this book included at least one character from Susan Stoker's books. To check out more, see below.

Rescuing Sadie (novella)
Rescuing Wendy
Rescuing Mary
Rescuing Macie (Novella)

Badge of Honor: Texas Heroes Series

Justice for Mackenzie (FREE!)
Justice for Mickie
Justice for Corrie
Justice for Laine (novella)
Shelter for Elizabeth
Justice for Boone
Shelter for Adeline
Shelter for Sophie
Justice for Erin
Justice for Milena
Shelter for Blythe
Justice for Hope
Shelter for Quinn
Shelter for Koren
Shelter for Penelope

SEAL of Protection Series

Protecting Caroline (FREE!)
Protecting Alabama
Protecting Fiona
Marrying Caroline (novella)
Protecting Summer
Protecting Cheyenne
Protecting Jessyka
Protecting Julie (novella)

Protecting Melody
Protecting the Future
Protecting Kiera (novella)
Protecting Alabama's Kids (novella)
Protecting Dakota

New York Times, USA Today and *Wall Street Journal* Bestselling Author Susan Stoker has a heart as big as the state of Tennessee where she lives, but this all American girl has also spent the last fourteen years living in Missouri, California, Colorado, Indiana, and Texas. She's married to a retired Army man who now gets to follow *her* around the country.

www.stokeraces.com
www.AcesPress.com
susan@stokeraces.com

Made in the USA
Monee, IL
10 January 2020

20141750R00144